I0725521

The Trouble with Mystery

A. R. Redington

Dovian's Journal: Gold Status Publishing

Dovian's Journal: Gold Status Publishing

www.ARRedington.com

Copyright © 2022 A. R. Redington

Original copyright © 2019 A. R. Crebs

First printing 2019 under the name A. R. Crebs.

All rights reserved. No part of this publication may be reproduced, distributed, or transmitted in any form or by any means, including photocopying, recording, or other electronic or mechanical methods, without the prior written permission of the author, except in the case of brief quotations embodied in critical reviews and certain other noncommercial uses permitted by copyright law.

Any references to historical events, real people, or real places are used fictitiously. Names, characters, and places are products of the author's imagination.

ISBN: 978-1-958038-03-1

BOOKS BY A. R. REDINGTON

The Esoteric Design

The Esoteric Design: Disbanding Hope

The Esoteric Design: Civilization Lost

Predator: Eyes of the Demon, The Trophy

Masters of the Ellem

The Trouble with Mystery

Whispers from Beyond: 30 Miniature Tales

DEDICATION

Dedicated to those who have stuck by my side and remain entertained by my ever-changing ideas and projects.

CONTENTS

AUTHOR'S NOTE

Never in my life did I think I would write a book like this. However, due to a fascinating stock image—used on the cover of this book—a plotline infected my brain. I shared the idea with some readers and friends and wrote it thanks to their encouragement. Here's to one more under the belt and many more to come. My desire to explore multiple genres continues to stir my imagination, and I hope you all remain entertained along the way.

CHAPTER ONE

Mystery. It's a thing I've always found intriguing. As simplistic as it may seem to others, the word contains an entire world within itself. It's unclassifiable, a thing that breaks free from the bonds of a simple explanation. Personified, Mystery is a riddle, an enigma that breathes life into the darkness surrounding all the questions. It demands curiosity, a critical need for exploration. Mystery holds a questioning existence, one that requires answers. It's random, exciting, beautiful, and deadly. There's an adrenaline rush that surrounds Mystery. The need to understand that which is mysterious is what drives me. That's why I packed up all my shit and moved to the big city a little over two years ago.

As I sat at the bar with my best friend, Liam—our Friday night routine—I was once again reminded of why I left my miserable small-town home in the Midwest. Where would I be if I hadn't? Probably barefoot and pregnant, making macaroni and cheese as my painfully boring husband sat on the couch drinking beer while watching the race on television. How anyone could find spectating cars as they sped in circles for half a day entertaining was beyond me.

The town I once resided in was about the size of a square mile and quiet, assaulted by blasting winds that covered everything with red dirt. I hated it.

The whole place smelled and looked filthy. It was barely big enough for a gas station and a small food market and offered little to no entertainment. There was a type of misery that clouded over the town. Poor men worked rough labor for horribly low wages and no benefits. Wives stuck to their homes and raised handfuls of children all by themselves. If the women did work, they either held a secretary position or drove to the neighboring towns to work at the clinics and retirement homes. It was peaceful in its own right, but after a while, I was dying to escape. There was no way of going up. And after assessing my past and current life and seeing nothing but dirty, drunk men and no possibility of bettering myself as the woman I wanted to be, I finally lost my mind.

My husband wasn't a bad guy. Mason was kind enough but had no ambition in life. He didn't want to do anything outside his daily routine—go to work, come home, and sit and stare at the television. I was scared of being committed to a man like that, knowing that my future consisted of preparing boxed dinners and having children to raise primarily by myself. So, I escaped. Our marriage wasn't perfect, but he did take the divorce surprisingly hard. I didn't know what he expected. As soon as the ring touched my finger, all of the date nights, flowers, holding hands, and passionate sex flew out the window. I had been claimed, and there was nothing else left for him to do. Mason had won his prize. And the fact that he was so surprised by my going aggravated me more. I used it as fuel to validate that I had made the right choice.

Thankfully, I have a college degree. A small-town girl with a thirst for more, I left that boring place after high school and received a degree in journalism. Unfortunately, I got trapped by marriage, and we returned to our native home, overwhelmed by crippling debt. However, as soon as we signed the divorce papers, I left that town, left the state entirely, and settled in one of the big cities over a twelve-hour drive away—a location I had always wanted to visit but never had the money to do so. Luckily, I snagged a job at a newspaper firm in the area. I got myself a lovely, overpriced, undersized apartment and quickly made friends with some of my new coworkers, one being Liam. He became my best friend, and I was okay with that. I didn't need an overabundance of people getting too close to me.

"Are you ever going to take a break?" Liam asked, tearing me away from my thoughts.

I flipped a page of the special edition magazine for our county, published by our newspaper firm. "I just want to make sure the editor didn't screw up my article. You know how much of an idiot she can be with words that don't fit her antiquated vocabulary," I said as I ran a finger over my article, skimming it.

"You referring to that time you wrote a story on anime culture, and she changed the word to anima throughout the article?" Liam hid his smile behind his beer bottle as he took a sip.

I irritably growled, turning to another page. "Yeah! Exactly! It made me look like an idiot! Like I didn't know what I was talking about."

Liam laughed. "Oh, that was when I discovered a fury like none other contained within little Zoey."

"I worked hard on that article. I watched a couple of episodes of the top-rated anime shows, attended a few of those comic cons, and had my picture taken with a bunch of scantily-clad chicks, sweaty men with weird wigs, and some furries." I shuddered at the thought. Honestly, it was a lot of fun. While researching for my article, I met several interesting people, but I also ran into a few creepers, which wasn't entirely surprising.

"Ah, furry culture. You know you like it." Liam grabbed the magazine from my hands, checking on his graphic design work. He made my article look clean and professional, incorporating some exciting banners and overlaid photos with my text wrapped around it. Liam always did an excellent job with my stories. Sometimes, I think he worked a little *too* hard on them, but that was how he operated.

"Right, I don't think anybody could get me into one of those mascot suits," I scoffed, grabbing my mixed drink.

"I think you'd look hella fine in a fox suit," he mumbled, curiously eyeing an advertisement.

I exhaled, trying my best to ignore his statement. Unfortunately, Liam also had the hots for me and wasn't shy about it. He frequently told me he was interested in dating, and this trend had occurred intermittently for the past couple of years. After several failed relationships, I decided that dating and marriage were not my thing. I found that everything immediately dulled as soon as a man had captured me. My partners were no longer fun or mysterious, and life suddenly became incredibly monotonous. That is, if we ever reached a relationship status between all the lies, cheating, and abuse.

I watched my coworker laugh with the bartender and ordered another beer. Liam had a charming smile and a full head of dark-brown hair that he cared for and sometimes styled. He often switched between trimmed facial hair or, like today, none at all. Both looks were appealing as he had masculine features and a chiseled jaw. Not only that, but Liam was a diligent worker, creative, funny, a talented actor on the side, and was good at various impersonations. He made me laugh and feel good and was a great therapist when I felt down. It seemed he fit the criteria of the perfect man, at least as close as a human could get to being perfect. I didn't want to ruin that. I did not want to lose the greatest friend I ever had. Getting into a relationship with him would destroy it all.

I gave him a suspicious look as he sniffed a page in the magazine. "What the hell are you doing?"

"Does this smell good?" He asked, shoving the advertisement in my face.

I cringed before realizing he was talking about a cologne sample made by a local company. Holding onto the magazine, I breathed in the scent.

"Yeah, that's actually nice. It doesn't smell like an old man or floor cleaner." I handed the item back.

Liam sniffed it again and then read the advertisement aloud. "Guaranteed to make her panties drop."

I leaned toward him, glanced at the page, and laughed. "It does not say that!"

He looked down at me with his grey eyes. "Would it make your panties drop?" he teased.

Without pause, I quickly tore out the cologne sample and rubbed it against his dress shirt. He made a shout of protest and quickly gave in, allowing me to cover him with the aroma. I then smelled his collar, feeling a tingle in my belly. It was amazing.

"Um, yeah. I think any guy who wears that could make my panties drop," I mumbled, drinking from my martini glass.

Liam's eyes widened, and his face turned a shade of pink. "Well…I know what I'm buying the next time I venture to the mall."

A loud crash caused me to jump. One of the servers behind us had toppled over a few glasses.

"Damn it! That's the third time this week!" The bartender, Ron, bellowed. He glared at the young man behind us and pointed to the kitchen. "Just get your ass in the back and start washing dishes. If I hear one more thing break, I'm sending your ass home, hear me?"

The waiter said nothing but sped behind the bar into the kitchen with his head downcast.

"Trouble with the help, Ronnie?" I asked.

Ron shook his head, his large hands resting on his hips. He was in his forties, bald, and covered in tattoos. "Eh, he's some med student training to be a nurse or something. You can tell he never worked a day in his life, but the guy needed some extra money, so I gave him some hours."

"Aw, that's so sweet," I mockingly stated.

Ron rolled his eyes. "Yes, I know, I'm far too nice. Maybe someday I can get some help that doesn't smash half my inventory into the floor within their first week."

Liam and I laughed.

"But it's a good thing I have you two," Ron continued. "You keep me in business well enough."

"Which reminds me," Liam said, "where's our mozzarella sticks?"

Ron's face paled only for a moment before turning red again. "You haven't gotten your order yet?" he snarled.

Liam gave a broad, tight-lipped smile and shook his head.

"Give me one moment," the bartender grumbled, shuffling back into the kitchen.

We suppressed our snickering.

After a second, Liam's eyes locked onto the screen above the bar. The television flickered to a breaking news story, the reporter detailing a rather gruesome report about a series of rapes and murders in the area. I cringed, and Liam wrinkled his nose.

"Ugh, can we change the channel? I have to hear about this crap all day from our coworkers. There's never anything positive going on during watercooler gossip." I searched the bar top, looking for the remote.

Liam snatched up a long metal stir stick, leaning over the side, and kept an eye on the kitchen. He carefully used it to poke a button to change the station. The mumbles of Ron commenced, and Liam quickly dropped the stick and sank onto his stool, groaning as he mockingly stretched his back.

"Here's your fried cheese," Ron grumbled. "Sorry about the wait."

"Aw, no problem!" Liam waved a hand dismissively. Eagerly, he snagged a mozzarella stick, shoved it in his mouth, and promptly spat it back out. "Ow, hot! At least they're fresh!" He grabbed his beer.

I picked up a stick and blew on it, watching the TV. Ron continued with his work, tending to other customers.

"Great choice of entertainment." I gestured toward the screen as I cleaned my new pair of dark-rimmed glasses with the edge of my shirt.

Liam raised his head and then snorted.

"Hey! It was better than that depressing shit they were showing. Graphic news doesn't make for a good date, does it?" He shrugged.

"And hand puppets do?" I raised an eyebrow.

Liam continued watching the afterschool children's show. A group of puppets danced in a circle, each spouting off a letter of the alphabet. I noticed movement beside me as Liam mimicked the colorful, fuzzy things. He swayed back and forth; his hands clenched into fists as he jiggled from side to side.

"Oh, my God! Stop it!" I hissed, slapping his shoulder.

"A is for...alcohol!" he said in a high-pitched voice as he lifted his beer. "B is for beautiful!" He slipped a finger through my blonde hair.

"This is why I can't take you out in public." I hid behind my hand.

"C is for cute!" He wrapped an arm around my shoulder. "D is for...." The man paused and then chuckled in my ear.

"Don't you even say it," I warned.

"Come on, Zoey. D is for...." This time, he spoke with a British accent. It was a tone he often used to frustrate me. What woman didn't like a proper British accent? At least it was better than his Scottish inflection, which he usually used after his third beer of the night. Liam was weird in a unique way, but it's why I liked him. He was hard to predict.

"Douchebag!" I cheered, pushing him away.

He sighed in defeat and ate another cheese stick. "You're never going to give me a chance, are you?" He looked disappointed.

I frowned, dipping my food in the marinara sauce. "Come on, Liam...you know I'm not into dating."

"But what do you call this?" He held out his hands. "EVERY Friday night?"

"Me hanging out with a friend."

"A male friend."

"I can't have male friends?" I asked.

"I just…" Liam hesitated. "I want to be more than that."

"Relationships are boring. Look at how we are right now; it wouldn't be like that. All the fun would disappear. Suddenly, we'd move in together. Then I'd be cooking your dinner, cleaning up after you, and soon we wouldn't even go out," I explained again.

"Zoey, I know you haven't had the best relationships in the past, but come on…I'm not like those other guys. We have fun together; you know it." He refused to make eye contact with me.

"Yeah, they all say that," I scoffed. "Listen, Liam. I care about you a lot. I really, really do. You are great. Perfect even! But I'm not a good fit for you. You need a good gal, someone who will stay committed. I'm not like that. I get scared off too easily. I don't want to hurt you like that. I'm a mess, and you know it wouldn't work out."

"Can't I decide for myself?" he asked, running a hand through his hair. "Can't we try, and I decide whether or not you're the gal for me?"

I chewed the chapped skin on my lip, not feeling awkward but guilty. The truth was, I wouldn't mind having Liam, but I didn't want him getting too attached. I wanted him as Liam, not as "mine." Though we knew a lot about each other, some things were left unsaid, unrecognized. There remained a bit of mystery behind the man, which kept him interesting. That was also what made him sexy.

"You know what?" I cleared my throat and looked around to ensure nobody would overhear our conversation. "I have an idea."

Liam looked up at me, hopeful.

"You know about my weird…fetish," I mumbled.

It wasn't necessarily a fetish, but I loved the idea of mystery—things left unspoken, subtle hints, exciting interactions.

"Yeah," Liam said quietly, his eyebrows lifting.

"What if you and I…did some…role-playing or something?" I suggested barely above a whisper.

"Role-playing?!" Liam blurted out with excitement.

"Shhh! Shut-up!"

The man quickly leaned closer toward me. "Yeah? I like the sound of that. Give me details."

I frowned, suddenly realizing how loud the bar had gotten. The dinner rush had arrived, and the servers were busy on the floor. Even the new guy walked by, asking if we needed anything else. Liam and I stammered a "no" with equal embarrassment. The young man quickly ducked away, and I abruptly returned my attention to my friend.

"Details!" Liam screeched.

"Okay! So…what if you and I…kind of…met up at my place at night?" I tugged on my hands, trying not to sound nervous.

"You…you want me to meet you at night?" he asked. "At your place? Like in your bedroom?"

"Well, yeah, but we must keep this a secret."

He frowned.

"I mean, what if you came dressed as a character?" It sounded more bizarre than I had intended.

"Character?" Liam questioned. "Like a hand puppet?"

"Come on now! I'm serious."

He nodded, allowing me to continue.

"You like to act. You're really good at it. Why don't you come up with a mysterious persona? Don't give me *any* details. I'll leave the door unlocked, and you can come over and surprise me." I gained a bit more confidence once I sputtered out the words. "It will be far from dull."

"Mysterious persona, eh?" A youthful grin spread over his face. "So, I get dressed up, all mysterious, and sneak into your apartment at night, and you and I...we...." A blush spread over his cheeks.

"We have mind-blowing sex." I nodded.

Liam covered his face, chuckling. "Are you insane?"

"No! You know how easily bored I get. Now, either you can play along, or you can say no to ever having sex with me." I folded my arms.

It was amusing how quickly his expression changed to dread at that threat. "Okay. I'll play along."

There were butterflies in my stomach, a thing I hadn't felt in years. I was nervous about the proposition but suddenly felt relieved after Liam agreed. I had hoped it would soothe some of the tension between us.

I held up a finger. "Only one stipulation." He eagerly nodded, and I continued. "You and I cannot speak of our normal lives while doing this. We are strangers. And, while we go about our ordinary, everyday lives, we cannot speak of our role-playing, got it?"

"Ohh, keeping secrets from our personas. I like it." He rubbed his hands together, his smile widening as the silence grew between us. I could tell he was already playing out scenarios in his head. "Okay...sounds exciting."

Liam seemed enthusiastic, indeed. His leg bounced as he ran his hands over his pant legs. Then, a dumbfounded look crossed his face, and he eyed me deviously. "Who do you want me to be?" he asked seductively. I grinned, liking his tone.

"You can be whoever you want to be," I whispered. "Surprise me."

"I can surprise you," he muttered, facing me. For a second, I was afraid he was going to kiss me.

"Who…who should I be?" I stammered.

"Just be you. A silent you."

"Silent?" I whispered.

"Just submit to the mystery man, and I'll be happy." He ran his finger along my collarbone.

I couldn't contain my excitement. I was more wound up than expected and decided it was time to leave.

Abruptly standing, I snatched up my jacket and purse and quickly finished my drink. "I'm going home," I hastily stated. "I…have things I need to get ready for."

"Oh!" Liam shook his head, handing his credit card over to Ron. "Um, yeah! Me too! I have an important meeting I need to get to." He coughed as he finished his beer.

I nodded.

Liam stood awkwardly before me. "Tonight?" he asked, rubbing the back of his neck.

"Yup!" I affirmed.

"Okay!" He fidgeted.

"Well, have fun at the meeting!" I waved and spun away, nearly running into the clumsy waiter Ron had previously yelled at. I heard a laugh from Liam, but I didn't look back, quickly exiting.

Once out of sight, I ran to my car. It's not something I'm proud to admit, but I felt like a child on her birthday. Suddenly, things with Liam just got a lot more interesting. I had no clue how I got home as my mind only thought of the exciting night I would have.

What was I going to wear? Did I shave that morning? Should I redo my makeup and hair? Would he find me sexy? Would this work out? One thing was certain: I was about to have a thrilling date with the one thing I desired most—Mystery.

CHAPTER TWO

By the time I arrived home, a cloud of drowsiness had overtaken me. Perhaps it was my nerves, or maybe the extra drink I had. Whatever it was, I wasn't about to let it ruin my plans.

As usual, I tossed my keys onto the counter, not bothering to lock the door behind me. Beelining to my coffeemaker, I gazed out the window above my sink. It was still daylight, so Liam would probably not arrive for a couple more hours. Actually, I had no idea when he would turn up, which meant I had to hurry. I started the brew and rushed to the bathroom. A quick shower and a closer, more personal shave wouldn't hurt. As I groomed myself, a million questions flew through my mind. Would he prefer me to be completely shaven? What did Liam expect? What if he didn't like my body? Looking attractive in clothes was quite different than being attractive while entirely naked. At least, in my eyes. My nerves struck again, and I stumbled to bed as I haphazardly slid on my robe. I still had to dry my hair and do my makeup. Would he want me all dolled up, or would he prefer I was all-natural and still wet from the shower?

The fresh scent of hazelnut coffee tickled my nostrils. A quiet purr alerted me to my warm, fluffy Hector curled up beside me. He was my fur-baby that I had adopted shortly after moving to the city. Liam often joked that Hector was the first piece to my crazy-cat-lady collection. I didn't mind the ridicule. Hector was my boy; he was gentlemanly, snuggled me every night, and was cleaner than most men I had dealt with in the past. Smiling, I closed my eyes as my black cat snuggled in, plopping against my side. Exhaustion overtook me, the room spinning. Perhaps a little nap wouldn't hurt. I left the door unlocked; Liam could let himself in. At this point, I didn't think he'd mind finding me wet and napping in nothing more than my bathrobe. Besides, I didn't plan to get much sleep once he arrived anyway. I hummed a laugh, petting Hector. His soothing purr, which I affectionately called his "sleeping pills," finally lulled me into a deep sleep.

A crash of thunder jolted me awake. Groggily, my eyes adjusted to the surrounding darkness. From my bedroom, I could see the pale light of the coffee maker.

"Oh, shit!" I looked over my bed, trying to find my phone. A blue light beaconed from my nightstand, and I pressed the button, quickly dimming the blinding light of the screen. It was eleven o'clock, and there was still no sign of Liam. However, I had a couple of messages.

'Hey, sorry, bad news. Got some flat tires. Will probably be really late. Gotta take the damn bus.'

I sighed. So much for keeping up the mystery of the game. Another message popped up.

'I hate myself. I somehow passed out on the bus. Missed my stop. I just got home.'

I groaned with dissatisfaction. Of course. Liam probably flaked out over the idea. I wrote back to him, *'No biggie. I fell asleep, too. Maybe another night. Codeword will be....'*

I thought for a moment. "Mystery," I said aloud with a smirk, typing into my phone.

'Gotcha. Reschedule for sure. And no more talking about it, right?' he quickly replied.

'Right. Gotta keep things interesting.'

'K. Definitely hate myself. For real. Feel stupid.'

'It's okay. No worries.' I huffed. I was slightly annoyed, but it wasn't his fault that he had some flat tires.

'If it makes you feel any better, I drooled all over myself and woke up leaning against a homeless man.'

I giggled. *'Ew. Take a shower.'*

'Yeah, headed there now. Care to join?' I could imagine his overconfident smirk.

I scoffed, clicking on my phone's keyboard. *'Already had mine. You missed out.'*

'For real? Damn.' A giant sad-face emoticon followed.

'For real. Anyway, I'm gonna get some work done.'

'Lame. It's the weekend.'

'Nothing better to do, right?'

'I suppose. Well, don't work too hard.'

'Never. Night.' I stared at the screen, waiting for his final reply.

Thunder cracked, the room lighting up for only a split second. From my peripheral, a shadow moved near the window. I jumped, holding a hand against my chest, a sharp yelp escaping me. Another flicker lit up the room, revealing the silhouette of a man.

"Oh, you scared me!" I laughed nervously. "You really had me fooled."

There was no response. I watched the figure, the silence heavy, and I cleared my throat. I had nearly forgotten that there was no speaking of our regular lives while in the bedroom. Everything had to remain shrouded in mystery.

"Mystery," I whispered. Then I remembered that Liam had told me to remain quiet during our game.

The man moved, his hand lightly drawing the curtain open a few inches, just enough to let in some pale light. He remained in the darkness, and we stared at each other in silent wonder. I hadn't the slightest idea what he was thinking, but I felt like an animal locked in the piercing stare of a hungry predator. I readjusted myself, sitting on the edge of the bed. My bathrobe hung loosely around my curves, the tie barely holding the center in place. The drumming rain calmed my nerves only a bit until he stepped into the light.

He stared at me with cold eyes from beneath the shadow of his hood. Dark soot surrounded them, which gave the illusion of hollow sockets. Inky lines of black and red stretched across his chiseled face, outlining each and every jagged curve. I remained frozen, locked in time, my mouth gaping as my breath failed to enter my lungs. He was frightening yet tantalizing in his mystery. And when he realized I made no motion to run, made not one single sound, his skeletal mouth twisted into a grin, the soft streetlight gleaming off his teeth. He was the image of death, yet his impression was strangely appealing.

My heart fluttered as he took a slow step forward. Curiously tilting his head, he continued to move slowly toward me. I remained in my place, excited, nervous, yet desperately intrigued. He made no sound but stood inches away. After his near-white eyes—contact lenses—searched my face for a moment, he slowly lifted a leather-gloved hand, timidly running his thumb and finger across my jaw. The scent of his cologne was slightly sweet and foreign, and I liked it. The barrage of new sensations made me dizzy.

I never thought Liam would be able to pull off something like this. His feral stare, how his lips parted as he rubbed his thumb against my lower lip, and the way he suddenly pulled me up and grabbed my waist made me insanely flustered. It wasn't supposed to be this easy, but it was.

He pressed his lips against mine and instantly divided them with his tongue. I didn't hold back, a soft moan escaping my throat. I could taste the paint on his lips and felt it smear onto mine. As he held me tight, his hands gripping my hips with need, I unconsciously responded by grinding against him. This elicited a breathy gasp from him. And I gave in at that one sound, the only noise he had made so far. Falling back onto the bed, I pulled on his shoulders, eagerly taking him against me. He didn't hesitate, and within moments, his fingers slipped through the opening of my robe, tracing along my inner thigh. I groaned, feeling high from his warm touch. I was ready and wanted him terribly.

At the sound of my pleasured moans, his lips finally left mine. He looked down at me, his icy eyes wandering over my face again. The painted mask he wore drove me mad. It was exactly as I had hoped. And the way he opened his mouth, breathing in sharply in anticipation as he slowly dipped his fingers inside of me, only drove me further into insanity. I was drunk on his look, on his mysterious features. And for a brief time, I nearly fell in love.

The first night was a near blur. It had gone so fast, yet some details remained fresh in my mind. We kept the lights off, which made sense not to ruin the illusion. Even our clothing remained on, though I was practically naked with my robe splayed open. I didn't protest; I loved running my hands beneath his clothing, getting only a trace glimpse of his toned body now and then as I felt up his shirt and tugged on his dark jeans. He moved slowly and slid off my glasses, carefully setting them on the nightstand.

We kissed most of the night. As I touched every curve and tight ridge beneath his clothing, I licked his lips, craving more. I imagined my mouth laid upon the areas of flesh my fingers traced. I nibbled his neck and collarbone, my hand teasing him through his pants. My breaths became quick and short, the excitement taking me to the edge before we even began. Though his erratic gasps only added to my pleasure, I held what little sanity I had until I couldn't bear to remain silent any longer. He had grown incredibly hard, his member twitching with his pulse. His thick hood was slick, only enticing me further.

"Please," I whispered.

He hesitated, his silver eyes smoldering with lust.

"I need to feel you," I said between bated breaths.

I wrapped my legs around his waist, trying not to lose myself as I felt his tip glide against me, teasing me. He said nothing, but his teeth grazed his lower lip as he heaved a loud sigh. And then, he pushed into me—only a bit at first.

I screamed. Not from pain but pure bliss. I had never been so turned on in my life. I clenched around him, pulling his hips against me with my legs, forcing him deep inside. Though slightly embarrassing, I finished without delay, quaking and squeezing him. I bit his shoulder, humming with each of his deep thrusts, my hands slipping behind him into his jeans to grip and pull him against me. I wanted him all; I needed to feel him completely. He didn't last much longer. With his fingers digging into my waist, he leaned forward, resting his forehead against the pillow, his mouth sucking on the base of my neck. I felt him spasm inside. Quiet, sharp exhales fled from him with each throbbing twitch, and he sank onto me, catching his breath.

We sat in the darkness, relaxed, our pants alternating. He remained buried inside me, and the two of us created shockwaves within one another as we rode out our high. After a minute, once the tingles subsided, he pushed up, sliding from me. I gasped at his exit, a series of incredible sensations tickling me once again.

"Oh, my God," I whispered.

He pulled up his pants and dropped to the side, staring at the ceiling. I was glad he didn't up and run, but now I was unsure of what to do next. Shrugging away the unease, I rolled toward him and snuggled against his chest, draping an arm over him.

He smelled like rain, sex, and that fantastic cologne. With a deep breath, I relaxed as I felt his tense body suddenly ease, and he cautiously wrapped an arm around me. I was drowsy before; the latest exercise had only exhausted me further. A sigh passed my lips, and I curled in closer, pulling the blanket around myself as I did so. Nearly asleep, I motioned awake at the feeling of the man's lips against my forehead. It was a sweet, soft gesture. And I smiled, as it was an act that I would expect Liam to do. Even playing the dark, bad boy, he couldn't hide his natural sweet side. It was comforting, and not long after, I fell asleep.

CHAPTER THREE

I awoke the following day to an empty space beside me in bed. I would've thought everything had been a dream except for the evidence left behind. As I entered the bathroom, I stared at my reflection in wonder. Smears of black covered my lips; touches of the mystery man's makeup tainted my skin along my neck and chest. Heat rushed to my face as I finally released my breath, my fingers tracing over the streaks. I couldn't help the smile that crept over my face.

"Wow," I whispered with a small laugh.

I noticed a text message from Liam I had missed. It said, *"Goodnight."*

"Sneaky boy." I grinned and set my phone on the counter by the sink.

After another quick shower, I wandered to the kitchen, frowning at the forgotten coffee pot. Nearly all the brew had evaporated, the kitchen smelling of burnt hazelnut. I dumped the sludge and set the pot to soak, annoyed that my coffee maker didn't have the auto-off ability. I needed one of those fancy coffee pod machines. Stretching, I eyed the oven clock and gasped. It was after noon already! How had I slept in for so long?

I groaned—my body ached all over. Feeling lazy and lethargic, I opted out of cooking for the day and ordered Chinese takeout instead, spending the rest of the evening eating gobs of unhealthy food and binge-watching films.

I started with a classic comedy and followed it up with a chick flick that gathered my curiosity. Usually, romantic movies weren't my type of thing, but this one had me crying like a baby. To even things out, after going through half a box of tissues, I grabbed some fruit snacks and found a paranormal thriller to watch. Ghost stories have always interested me, including anything involving extraterrestrials or strange beings. I wasn't much into bigfoot, though.

I grew tired of watching movies and grabbed my phone, checking on my mobile games. A growl vibrated in my throat when I noticed one of my villages had been burnt to the ground overnight by a rival clansman's dragon. I clicked the notification to see who had done it and furiously began messaging the one responsible.

'Okay, NinjaWarrior86, you're a dick.'

I cleaned up my village, fed my townspeople, and ran a few puzzles to help incubate a dragon egg of my own. He would be ruined after thirty minutes once the egg hatched.

'MWAHAHA! Shouldn't have gone MIA for three days,' he replied.

'I'll let you know; I am currently growing an Emerald Fire dragon. Your village is doomed.'

It took a few minutes before another reply came through.

'Black dragon incoming. ETA forty-five minutes.'

I gasped. "Don't you dare, Liam!" I shouted.

'Motherfucker. If you do....' I typed.

'You gonna punish me?'

'I'm gonna pillage your entire village and steal all your women and children.'

We played until our credits ran out, and then we challenged each other to a few rounds of Word Mashup, which I won, of course. After the third playthrough, Liam challenged me to a few games of pool, where our skills were more evenly matched.

'Hey, it's getting late. I still have to hit up the gym,' he messaged me.

'Okay! Get it done!' I inserted a couple of emojis with flexing arms.

'Talk to you later!'

'Night!'

I played on my phone for a while, checked messages, read articles, and then grinned when another game notification appeared. My Super Elite Rainbow dragon had hatched. I sent it to Liam's village and burnt the entire thing to the ground, stealing all his warriors and resources. I cackled like a villain. He most likely wouldn't see it for another hour or two.

Before I knew it, it was after midnight. I admit I felt guilty for being so lazy, but then again, I wanted to reward myself after the night before. Even though I wasn't tired, I knew I would screw up my sleep schedule if I stayed up much longer. That was the one thing I hated most about the typical workforce. Being a natural night owl, getting up early in the morning to clock-in at eight was something I always struggled with. Thankfully, my boss understood and allowed me to push my schedule back. As long as I completed my work each week, she didn't mind when I came in closer to nine. Besides, I was salary. I worked more than enough hours while on vacation and at home, one perk of being a writer. Writing gave me more independence than the designers had, like Liam. The poor guy always ran a tight schedule. At least he was a morning person.

After turning off the television and tossing my trash, I headed to the bathroom to prepare for bed. If anything, I could read a book. That usually made me sleepy. A gust of wind slammed against the side of the building, causing a loud creak. I jumped at the sound.

"Okay, no more ghost stories," I grumbled as I washed my hands.

Stretching, I strolled into my bedroom. Wearing pajamas was the norm for my weekends. If I didn't have anywhere to go, you bet your ass I wasn't going to dress up. Hector chirped as I removed my pants, and he dashed past me into the living room. I eyed him, giggling at his crazy Halloween cat pose.

"What're you doing, scary boo?" I asked him. "Did that scary movie get ya worked up?"

Hector's eyes stared past me as his tail fluffed. A sudden chill ran down my spine. From my current angle, I had a clear view of the entry to my apartment. The door remained unlocked. I spun and came face-to-face with the mystery man.

I yelped as he gripped my shoulders and roughly pushed me onto the bed. I could barely protest before he climbed over me, his hands running over my body, his lips pressing against mine. Humming into his kisses, I instantly felt a flutter in my stomach and heat between my thighs. Two nights in a row? I certainly wasn't expecting that.

His actions were more forceful this time, but I didn't mind. The scent of his cologne tickled my senses, along with the musty smell of booze. Liam must've been drinking at Ronnie's earlier while we were gaming and got a bit frisky, using the gym as an excuse to trick me. The thought made me giggle, but he quickly swallowed the sound with his tongue. He pinned my wrists above my head, grinding against me. I could barely contain my eagerness. He was hard, and as he pressed his hips to mine, I felt the warm twitch of his pulse against my thigh. I wrapped my legs around him, wanting more.

His hot breath warmed my neck as he sucked my skin. Not wanting to ruin the façade, I removed my glasses, and everything blurred as I reached underneath his hood, careful not to remove it, running my fingers through his hair. His body tensed, and he touched my face, covering my eyes. I quickly lowered my hands. Slowly, his lips grazed my ear.

"Keep 'em closed, love," his husky voice rumbled with a slight British accent.

I gnawed my lip, tightening my thighs. The mysterious man returned my hands to his head, letting me grip his hair. He removed his hood.

"No peeking," he said in a commanding voice, "or I'll have to punish you." I whimpered in response.

Slowly, he trailed kisses down my neck, moving lower to my chest. I gasped as his teeth grazed my nipple through my tank top. He gave a quiet growl, lifted my shirt, and planted his mouth over my left breast. I nearly bit through the skin of my lip as I snarled in return. He was so bold. I loved it.

Combing my fingers through his hair, I submissively held on with my eyes closed. I let my hands tell the story as his body lowered with each kiss and nibble. His tongue swirled around my belly button, and I suppressed a snicker, unconsciously raising my hips. His teeth gently scraped against my skin as he smiled at my response. To know he was having so much fun with my body only made me hotter. I liked this version of the usually passive Liam. It was a side I had never known.

My mind went blank as I felt his fingers slide through the side of my panties. I was already wet. It didn't take much to get me going during our game, which was surprising. He toyed with me, circling my bud, his fingers tracing along my entrance. And my thoughts stopped again as he removed the undergarment and quickly pressed his mouth in its place. A gasp escaped my throat, and I tightened my grip as he kissed and sucked my sensitive parts. His fingers slowly entered me, and my thighs clenched around his head.

Fighting to stay silent, I alternated between pulling his hair and grinding my hips. I had to admit that I wasn't entirely used to it. Oral sex, for me, hadn't been pleasant in the past. In fact, most of the men I knew hated returning the favor, other than a couple of sex fanatics who I would never consider allowing the pleasure of sharing my bed. At least, my exes either hated it or were terrible at it. Because of this, I was a bit self-conscious about the act, but by keeping my eyes closed, my anxiety quickly dissipated.

The man was amazing.

As he continued his ministrations, I felt myself climb to the edge. My breaths quickened, and so did his pace. I squirmed, wanting more, craving more. After thinking of our first time together, my legs trembled as I desired to have him fill me once again. The thought alone was enough to send me closer to climax. My legs constricted around him as I fought against the urge. He grunted and removed his fingers, gripping my thighs instead. I exhaled, both happy and disappointed at his slight pause. Of course, I wanted nothing more than to orgasm at once, but I also didn't want to finish that way. I needed him deep inside. I desired to feel his trembling release within me.

I pouted as he parted and trapped my thighs with his forearms and hands. His mouth took over, licking and probing. I couldn't help but fight against his hold, the tingling heat quickly building inside once again. Words lost, I whined, but it was a noise he understood as I didn't want to go just yet. He grinned against me and only quickened his pace. I let out a small scream.

"That's it," he hummed.

The sound of his voice and the sensations were dizzying.

"I…not yet," I panted.

He ignored my protest and continued. Another squeak passed my lips, and my legs fought against his hold. I was losing control, wriggling in his grasp.

"Yeah," he whispered. "Come on."

"No." I shook my head, feeling playfully stubborn.

"Do it."

My head shook again.

"Yes," he growled. "Cum for me."

I couldn't breathe, I couldn't hold still, and I couldn't fight it any longer. My heavy pants turned into tiny yelps.

"That's it. Now. Cum."

Oh, his delicious voice, methods, scent, and warmth. Everything pushed me past my limit. I tried to pull away as everything became too intense. My back arched as I came. I would've felt bad for tugging his hair so sharply, but

I didn't care at that moment. Besides, he seemed to enjoy it, giving a pleasured hum as he vigorously kept his momentum. I let out a sharp cry. Screw my neighbors and everyone within the square block who probably heard me. This was my fantasy. Modesty be damned, I was going to enjoy it fully.

As I descended from my high, my heavy breaths were the only sound in the room. He removed his lips and quickly replaced his hood. I hadn't even noticed that I opened my eyes. I was too preoccupied with other things to care. He climbed to lay beside me, his fingers gently rubbing between my legs as I rode out the last quakes. I stared into his near-white eyes, intrigued by the contact lenses that gave him the spooky appearance. Still, his identity remained secret, hidden in the darkness and makeup smears.

"Hm. I didn't want to go so fast," I whispered.

"I wanted you to," he quietly replied.

"But…" I hesitated, "what about you?"

"Oh," he chuckled deeply. His gaze flew to his hand as he applied more pressure to his massage. I inhaled sharply. "Don't you worry, love. You're all mine tonight."

"All night?" I gave a nervous giggle. I couldn't believe his effect on me.

He leaned down toward me. "We're just getting started," he hissed, his lips skimming mine. Then, he kissed me deeply, passionately.

I grew more intoxicated with each caress, and before I knew it, I craved him all over again. He undid his dark jeans and covered my body with his. I immediately reached inside his sweater to touch his hot skin. His warmth, his aroma, his voice, everything—I craved it all.

"You're mine," he whispered against my throat.

"Uh, huh." I nodded with a gasp.

He slipped inside of me without warning, pressing his forehead against mine. My insides squeezed tightly around him, and he let out a soft moan. His thrusts were slow at first, but the pace soon quickened. From the feel of his movements and flexes, I knew he wouldn't last long. I decided to help, rolling my hips against him, making sure to swirl his tip before pulling him deep inside. A soft gasp slipped from him, his fingers digging into my hip. I grinned, and he gave a feral snarl.

"Cheeky girl." He plunged deep, making me squeal.

I returned the gesture, and we alternated hard and soft thrusts.

"Damn it," he said between closed teeth as his eyes clenched shut.

"Cum for me," I whispered in his ear.

He made a noise, nearly collapsing on me, and he plunged further, pulling my hips up and forcing me against him. I felt his tip deep within, and I cried out from the sudden sharp movement. The sound must have been the final straw as he came, holding me tight. I rolled gently against him, supporting myself so he'd remain fully inside. His spasms hit just the right spot, and the sensations began to build once again. Silvery eyes settled on mine, and he watched with a lustful stare as he gyrated against me, pressing a hand gently against my lower abdomen.

"Oh, God!" I gasped, grinding my hips.

"Is that the spot?"

"Ye-yeah." I could barely speak.

He moved back just an inch and plunged again, making me shriek. How dare he make me orgasm so quickly a second time. My competitive side kicked in. I sat up and wrapped my legs around his waist. He knew what to do, palming underneath me as I sat upon his lap. I bounced with his support, feeling him wholly. Latching my mouth onto his neck, I pulled on the collar of his hoodie to gain better access, my tongue swirling in circles. It must have been a sensitive spot, for he moaned and tensed, his fingers pinching me. Pleased by his sounds, I sucked on the soft skin and gave occasional bites. We tightly held one another, exploring each other's delicate areas. As his breaths tickled the right side of my neck, I gave a breathy laugh, ecstatic from all the pleasure he gave me.

"You're amazing," he mumbled. His arm wrapped around me, forcing me into a snug embrace, his face buried in my neck.

"Almost," I gasped as I felt my pleasure build.

"Yeah?" His tone had changed from warm and soft to confident once again.

"Yeah," I confirmed with a short nod.

He sucked hard on my neck near the top of my collarbone. That was going to leave a mark. A heavy breath passed through his nose. "Yeah." He nodded in return.

"You too?" I asked.

He didn't respond, but his pace changed. I chanted 'yeah' with each rise of my nearing orgasm. He soon joined, and we alternated in beats. Within a few more thrusts, I could barely keep my breath, and I gave a silent scream as I reached my peak. His strong arms clamped tightly around me in a near-painful hug as he followed with another of his own. I moved slowly against him as he carefully placed soft kisses along my shoulder. We rode out the high for a few minutes. I felt weak, exhausted, and desperately out of shape.

Slowly, we detached, both slick with a sheen of sweat. I dropped back onto the mattress, giving a loud sigh. I was surprised to see him collapse next to me and pull me where my back faced him. He wrapped an arm around me, and we spooned. I wiggled a bit to get comfortable in his embrace. I honestly enjoyed the caring gesture.

"Tired, already?" I asked.

"Hmm, maybe just a little nap before the next round." His husky voice continued to give me chills.

I gave a tired laugh. "So…mysterious man. What shall I call you?"

There followed a moment of silence. "Mystery…" he paused, "I kind of like the sound of that."

"So, Mr. Mystery…or Mr. 'E?'" I wrinkled my nose.

"Does sound a bit like a cheesy villain, doesn't it?" he mused.

"Ah, yeah."

"How about we leave off the mister part, yeah?"

"Still sounds like Mr. 'E' no matter what."

"I feel like we're putting too much thought into this." He chuckled. The sound vibrated my ear.

"Well, what else am I supposed to say when I cry out in pleasure?"

His teeth nipped my earlobe. "Call me what you want, love. Or call me Mysterious."

"Mysterious." It worked. It wasn't casual and awkward like "Bob" or "Randy" and still felt proper for our game. "Okay, *Mysterious.*"

Sleep overcame me as he gently stroked my hair. Oh, how did he know that was one of my favorite things? Liam, or Mysterious, paid far too much attention to every detail I had ever given him. It was cute and exciting, but the thought made me cringe inwardly. It would have come across as creepy if I hadn't been his closest friend these past few years.

"You're lucky you're cute, Mysterious," I sleepily muttered.

"Oh?" he quietly replied.

"I let you get away with far too much." Yawning, I swiftly fell asleep to the sound of his soft laughter and warm embrace.

Work on Monday was undoubtedly going to be interesting.

CHAPTER FOUR

Monday morning arrived, and I found it hard to get out of bed. Perhaps I was more out of shape than I thought; maybe the sex was just that good, but I wanted nothing more than to punt my alarm clock across the room and sleep in. I sat up, stretched, and sighed with a groan as my spine cracked in multiple places. I eyed the spot next to me. It was as if no one had been there; the pillow remained straightened, and the covers were neatly tucked in. I knew last night wasn't a figment of my imagination. I never bothered to make my bed. Oh, what a sweet gentleman Mysterious was. It was an amusing thought.

A loud meow came from the floor.

"Oh, goodness! Are we starving to death?" I asked Hector.

Dilated pupils rimmed in green stared at me from below. "Meow!"

"Really?"

"MEOW!" Hector casually turned, heading for the kitchen, his tail straight in the air.

"Sassy bastard."

Mornings were evil; there was no doubt about it. And it seemed it was about time I started running the heater at night. It was freezing! I grabbed my robe and conducted my morning routine, making sure my furry asshole of a cat received his breakfast first. As I plodded back and forth around the apartment with as little enthusiasm as a child forced to go to school, Hector watched me from the back of the couch, his fur matching the dark fabric.

"Coffee? No, brush your teeth first. No, coffee first with a snack, and then brush your teeth." I eyed the clock and heaved a sigh. "Teeth first. Bring coffee and breakfast with you to the office." Speaking to myself aloud was a bad habit, but it sometimes kept me on track with the task at hand. Getting lost in my mind was why I arrived late to work each morning.

After a circle around my apartment, my aggravation got the best of me. "Where the fuck are my shoes?!" Oh, they were kicked under the bed.

I laced up my sneakers, a style that irritated my boss to no end as it seemed unprofessional, and then reached for my leather jacket.

"Hoodie?" I eyed the weather report on my phone. "Jacket."

Luckily, there wasn't any ice, so I didn't need to waste more time defrosting my car, but damn, it was cold. I ran the heater full blast and glared miserably out the windshield, berating myself again for not considering a remote start for my vehicle.

I shivered as my mind swirled with cliché ideas for my next article. It was soon time to appeal to the masses, writing about holiday decorations, gift ideas, recipes, etc. It was easy work for the most part, but I always tried to find a way to make my stories more unique than the millions of others covering the same themes. As I drove, my head spiraled with ideas.

"Holiday gifts even your mother-in-law would love. Lame! A strange gift for the strange person in your life. Possibly. Nerdy gifts? Gamer gifts? Gifts for people who have the personality of a doorknob? No, way too difficult."

I sipped my coffee as I waited in traffic.

"Gifts for that sex god in your life?" I laughed to myself. "What would that even be? Would you give him gifts he would want to use on himself or something to use on me? Save that idea for Valentine's Day," I noted.

The drive took twice as long as usual. It seemed everyone was having the same Monday I was.

"Fuck Mondays," I growled as I slammed my car into park. I would have to make an excuse for why I was so late. Sure, I didn't have to show up first thing in the morning, but this was a bit excessive.

"Hi, Zoey!" the sales rep cheered as he held the door open for me. The man was obnoxiously chipper in the mornings. Liam and I joked that he put cocaine in his morning coffee.

"Hey. How's it going?" I politely replied.

"Ah, same old, same old! Gotta get those ads sold for the 'Holiday Special!'" He laughed and chewed on his pen like it was a cigarette.

I nodded and waved as I entered while he exited the building. Of course, the ads were often sold nearly a month ahead of the specialized publications. Liam would spend many hours building the issue with Autumn colors and cheesy Fall leaf and pumpkin clipart. He loved designing for special editions. At least someone enjoyed this time of year with the company.

I said hello to my coworkers, rushing down the hall to my small office, which was more like a cubicle.

"Zoey! I've been looking for you."

"Ah, shit," I quietly whispered before I turned.

I tried to avoid my boss, but she occupied the stall beside mine, grilling a coworker about their sports editorial.

"Hey, Maria," I said with a forced smile.

The tall, robust middle-aged woman enjoyed wearing dark pantsuits with outdated shoulder pads, looked like she smoked too much in her younger years, and had puffy light brown hair. Her best accessory was her cold demeanor and permanently tight lips.

"Coming in a bit late today." It wasn't a question, just a short statement. Maria smirked at me, but I could tell she was annoyed. I could have told her

I wasn't feeling well or blamed traffic, but that never worked.

"Ah, yes, sorry. I was heading out the door when I noticed I had missed a call from Santa Steve," I lied.

"Already?" she asked.

"Yeah, he wanted to ensure we would run the story on him and the charity again this year."

Maria rolled her eyes. "We always do!"

I shrugged. "I know. You know how he is: always excited about playing Santa and gathering donations. I think he will do a pre-Christmas thing at the mall for Thanksgiving."

Maria nodded. "We should probably cover that as well."

"I told him I would chat with you about it and then give him a call back once I was in the office. Nothing is set in stone. He said it was some last-minute idea he had."

"Well, if he does, go ahead and cover the event. It would be a nice prep story for the holiday release." Maria shuffled some papers in her hands. "And what's on the agenda for today?"

I pondered, thankful the subject of my being tardy had been avoided. "I'm going to go over the 'Holiday Special' ideas. The typical stuff. Trying to think of something a bit more unique."

"Are you covering the bonfire tonight at the college?" she asked, her eyes not lifting from her stack of papers.

"Uhhh, am I?" I had forgotten about the big rivalry game. "I don't usually do sports."

"No, Ben's covering the game, but we need someone to cover the pregame celebration."

Each year, it was a tradition for the rivaling teams to host a large bonfire before the game, where they burned stuffed animals of each other's mascots and chanted insults in retaliation. Barbeque and beer served in excess often caused a ruckus among the students in the parking lot. I thought of how cold it was outside and wrinkled my nose. I hated outdoor events.

"Gotcha. Yeah, I'll snap some pics."

"Six-thirty tonight," Maria replied.

"Okay."

"I'm gonna head out for a while. Keep an eye on everyone. Call my cell if you guys need anything."

I nodded and settled into my desk space. For some reason, Maria still trusted me to monitor the office. I may have been a bit late most days, but it didn't mean I didn't do my job. I was one of the quickest writers and could churn out multiple stories with word counts high enough to cover numerous pages daily. In fact, I had to cut down on my content as we had an overabundance of filler stories at our disposal. Besides, I didn't make as much fuss when given assignments as others did.

I enjoyed the work. The only thing I didn't like was the constant drama from my coworkers. One pastime remained consistent while working in the news and media world: spreading gossip and rumors. Chatter extended from typical politics to the personal lives of fellow employees. I mostly stayed out of it. I learned early on not to participate in such catty activities. If I were to join in, I could easily get carried away, and alternate versions of my past would surface through the halls, even childhood rumors I never knew. Funny how that happens.

Staring at my computer monitor, I could feel my eyes glazing over with boredom and lack of creativity. All I could think about was the weekend and the fun physical activities I had experienced. I groaned and buried my face in my hands.

"Don't you love Mondays?" a familiar voice asked.

I looked up, sighing in aggravation toward Liam. "Monday can die, but then Tuesday would take its place."

Liam's area was on the opposite side of the building. Still, he always found an excuse to come to my end to harass me for a few minutes. I was always thankful for the distraction. Sometimes, being alone with my thoughts for hours on end was more destructive than constructive.

"Coffee?" he asked.

I eyed my thermos and took a long sip. It wasn't even half empty, but I decided I could use a break. As I walked beside Liam, the scent of his cologne filled the air.

"Mmm, new smell?" I asked.

Liam eyed me in confusion, and then his eyes widened. "Oh! Me?" he asked.

"Yeah." I leaned toward him and sniffed his dress shirt. The realization hit me. "Smells familiar," I said as I cleared my throat. "It's very, uh, mysterious."

Liam laughed. "Mysterious? Heh. It's from that advertisement, remember?"

"Ah, yes, while at the bar."

"Remember what you said about it?" He smirked.

"The scent would make my panties drop?"

"Yup! Sooooo?" He gaped at me.

"What?"

"Did they?"

I couldn't hide my broad grin as I sniffed him again. "Mmm, good thing I'm not wearing any today."

He nearly stumbled as we entered the break room.

"Well," he hesitated and cleared his throat, "how was your weekend?"

I looked away so he wouldn't notice my blush and started a pot of coffee. "Oh, it was pretty good."

"Oh, yeah? That's good."

"Great, actually. I rather enjoyed it." I brushed my hair behind my ears and refused to make eye contact. Why was I so nervous all of a sudden?

"Anything I should know about?"

"Just lots of Chinese food, movies, and…exercise."

"Wow, sounds somewhat more productive than my weekend."

I fiddled with the coffee maker, pouring in extra water. "Oh? What did you do?"

"Stayed in bed, mostly…but I did manage a workout last night."

I laughed. "Yeah, yeah."

"Was *so* tired this weekend for some reason."

"Me, too."

Liam smirked. "I'm sorry about Friday night."

"What do you mean? It was fantastic…." I paused. We weren't supposed to talk about it. "I mean, I always love hanging out with you."

"Well, my damn flat tires kinda ruined it. By the time I got home, it was so late."

"Heh, that's okay. Everything turned out fine. You know, I thought you had flaked out on me for a minute."

Liam frowned. "I'd never. Sometimes life just…gets in the way."

"Yeah. But anyway, top-secret, remember?"

He nodded. "Ah, right, right. But one thing, really quick, so we're on the same page."

My brow raised. "Yeah?"

"Shall we continue…" Liam peered over each shoulder as if he expected eavesdroppers, "Codename: Mystery?"

A burst of laughter exploded from me. "Ha! Um…yeah. I am *definitely* down with continuing."

His face reddened, and he chuckled while running a hand through his hair. He took a quick breath and eyed the hallway once again.

"My, my…suddenly so shy?" I ran a finger up and down his chest, biting my lower lip.

Like a switch, his eyes darkened, and he leaned down. "Me? Shy? With you?" A vibration of laughter escaped him. "Not with my little Zoey."

I quickly turned to refill my thermos. "Good! Now, no more talking about it."

In agreement, he nodded, but his smoldering stare remained. I fidgeted, eyeing him. He always dressed well and cared for himself physically, but Liam wasn't a complete fitness nut. He had the guilty pleasure of indulging in microbrews and gourmet burgers a bit too often. Still, he suddenly appeared so much more appealing after our secret weekend.

"So, are we doing lunch today?" He thankfully changed the subject before I decided to molest him right then and there.

"Yeah. If you want." It was a common occurrence. "I didn't bring any lunch, so I figured we'd catch the special at the café across the street."

"Chicken dumpling soup is the special today, and I could smell her freshly baked cinnamon rolls."

"Yes," I agreed, not needing to hear any more details. The warm soup would be perfect for such a frigid day.

"And I bet she's got the pumpkin spice going by now."

I giggled. Yes, I loved pumpkin spice everything. To add to the stereotype, I also had terrible dance moves, to which Liam often teased me.

"Liam! Ya gonna get that cover designed, or are you going to flirt with your girlfriend all day?"

Liam turned toward the door, stammering. "Ah, yeah! I was just running some ideas through Zoey."

His coworker, Josh, gave him a skeptical look. "Uh, huh. Hi, Zoey." He was a middle-aged man with black and grey hair. He wore frumpy clothing and had a bit of a belly but always donned a charming smile and had a witty sense of humor.

I wiggled my fingers in greeting. Josh always teased Liam and me from the first day we met. Initially, his jokes embarrassed Liam, but Josh's antics at least provided entertainment throughout the day. As time passed, Liam smiled in agreement as he made it clear when he eventually became interested in dating me. I, on the other hand, went with the flow. I wasn't offended but sometimes rolled my eyes when the harassment was too much. Even though I wasn't keen on relationships, flirting was always fun, at least with Liam. I felt safe with him.

"Okay, okay," Liam filled his mug with the hot brew. "Lunch." He pointed a finger at me.

I bobbed my head. "Lunch."

Liam turned to Josh. "You joining us today?"

Josh dismissively waved a hand. "Naw, I'm meeting the old lady today."

Married, Josh spent his lunches either eating at his desk, with us, or sometimes with his wife. The couple lived plainly, their marriage not one that craved fanciful attention or a need to keep up with the Joneses. Josh and his wife shared a sense of humor and were down-to-earth.

"All right, then. Later, Zoey." Liam cleared his throat and gave me a subtle wink. I couldn't suppress my smile. I quickly shook away my thoughts and cleaned up my coffee mess. I had work to do, and I was already far behind schedule.

The rest of the day and week went along as usual. Liam met up with me during breaks. We had our regular conversations, each growing bolder with our flirtations. I never intended to entice Liam further while at work, at least nothing more than was typical, but I was too damned excited about our game. I was a little disappointed that he hadn't visited me during the workweek, but it was understandable. It probably wouldn't be a bright idea to sleep together on a work night. I didn't want him to worry about staying at my place and sneaking out, running on little sleep. Also, it would ruin the theme if he were to stay the night and we went to work together. Something about him wearing the clothes from the day before smelling like sex while walking into the office at my side didn't seem as enticing as it would be embarrassing with the way the office gossiped. However, I suddenly looked forward to the weekend for the first time in ages.

My body greatly betrayed me by Friday. Just the thought of having a sexual encounter made me wiggle with anticipation. I also caught myself countless times biting my lower lip as Liam and I chatted, my eyes scouring his form beneath his neatly cut clothes. Why was he suddenly fifty times more attractive to me?

"You feeling all right?" Liam's question broke me out of my daze.

"Huh? Yeah, yeah! Fine. Why?" I removed my gaze from him and focused on the television above the bar as I sipped my martini.

"You keep staring off into space. Or…maybe you're just staring at me." He took a drink, trying to hide his smug grin.

"Mmm, maybe I've just got a lot of stuff on my mind."

"I can't imagine what that would be?" He faced me, resting his elbow on the bar with his cheek against his fist.

"LOTS of things."

He leaned toward me, and I caught a whiff of his scent. I instinctively clenched my thighs together, tearing my teeth across my glossed lip, now slightly swollen with how often I pulled at it.

"You know, if you keep doing that, I will have to do something about it." I shivered at his deep voice.

"About what?" I asked.

"You sucking on your lip like that."

He grew braver by the minute, his confidence rising after a couple of bottles of beer.

"Oh?" I matched his tone. "And what are you going to do about it?"

His mouth lingered dangerously close to my earlobe. "My lips are feeling a bit jealous. Why don't you give them a try?"

My chest heaved with my sudden erratic breaths. Oh no, I wanted to kiss him so badly. Already? Was I already giving into him? I had to calm myself and take control.

"Hmm, you would like that, wouldn't you?" I asked as I placed my hand on his upper thigh, running a finger lightly across his pants. I felt a twitch, could tell he was already growing hard, and imagined him deep inside me, pulsing, moaning.

Clearing my throat, I quickly pulled my hand away, lifting my drink again.

"Last weekend was so much fun," I sighed. "I certainly hope this weekend goes well."

Liam suddenly looked flustered. "I imagine it would have been better if my tires weren't slashed."

"Is that fixed yet?" It turned out that his tires actually were flat that night, but he was a true champ for following through with our game despite the inconvenience.

He nodded, shifting in his seat to readjust himself. "Yup. Gotta pick it up first thing in the morning before I head out."

"Head out?"

Liam rolled his eyes. "Yeah. I promised my sister I would help with my niece's birthday party."

"Doesn't she live a few hours away?"

"Yup. So...I'll be staying with her this weekend."

My heart dropped into my stomach.

"Oh. Well...that sounds...fun," I mumbled.

Liam sighed. "I could take you with me if ya want."

I laughed. "Ha! And meet your family and hang out with the kids? No.

No, I'm good."

He rubbed the back of his neck. "Figured you wouldn't want to tag along. Oh, well. Your loss."

I frowned, taking a big gulp from my glass. "You're telling me."

"But it's a good thing. You'd just make fun of me."

"Why?"

"Cuz she wants me to dress as a clown."

I nearly spit my drink all over the bar. "What?!"

Liam cringed.

"You're going to be a clown this weekend?" I cackled.

"My niece likes this stupid kid's show with this annoying clown. And with my acting experience, my sister thought I would be perfect. I denied her repeatedly, but then she made me feel guilty by sending a video of her daughter cheering for joy over the news that Clacky the Clown would make an appearance."

I gasped. "That bitch."

Liam gave another loud exhale. "Yup. So that's how I got roped in."

"You must take photos."

"I'm sure my sister will take hundreds and spread them all over the internet like some venereal disease."

"Clacky the Clown does kind of have an STD ring to it."

Liam snickered and gave me a strange look, grinning wildly. "Sexy, eh?" he asked in a terrible cockney accent.

I shook my head, cringing. "Nope."

"Aw, come on, Zoey! Once you have Clacky, you never go backy!" He added a horrifying clown laugh.

"Oh, God! Does he really sound like that?" I couldn't help the expression of disgust that crossed my face.

"Yup!" he shouted in the annoying voice.

"Nope, nope. Not sexy. At all."

Liam's laughter quickly died down. "That's right. You only like the *proper* British accents."

I eyed him from my peripheral.

"Isn't that right, love?" he whispered near my ear.

I stiffened; my hormones were raging once again. "You'd best be careful, mister."

And we had gone full circle once again, locked in each other's lustful stare.

"Careful?" He tickled my knee. "And don't you mean *mysterious?*"

"Don't start what you can't finish," I warned.

I was beyond irritated that he was busy for the weekend.

"Well, the bathrooms here are quite spacious," he suggested.

I wrinkled my nose. "Hell no."

"Come to my place?" he asked.

I quirked an eyebrow. "Sorry, I may have a date with *Mysterious* tonight."

"Ah, yes." He looked off to the side. "Mysterious," he grumbled, sounding a bit sour.

"You don't like the idea?" I suddenly felt nervous about his reaction.

"No, I'm just jealous of this Mysterious character." He winked.

I laid my cash out on the bar and stood. "Well, I'm heading home. Going to slip into something more comfortable."

"Like?"

Failing to make a seductive expression, I whispered, "My bathrobe and bunny slippers."

"Mmm, hot."

"If I don't see or hear from you again, have fun this weekend." I pushed in my chair.

Liam swirled the bit of beer left in his bottle.

"And I want to see pics!" I pointed at him.

"I'm sure you will." He rolled his eyes and cleared his throat. "Well, have a good night. I'll…see ya later."

Nodding, I exited, saying goodbye to the bartender, Ron. The night air cut through me, and I cinched my coat tightly as I looked through the bar window. Liam finished his beer and slapped his money on the counter. As I rounded the corner, he swept his coat around his shoulders. It seemed he was as eager as I. Anticipation rose, and my tummy fluttered. Liam may have had plans for the weekend, but he had tonight at least to play with me. I nearly skipped to my car, rushing inside to crank the heat.

CHAPTER FIVE

ow I love surprises. The disappointment of Liam staying with his sister over the weekend only made Mysterious' appearance even more exciting and pleasurable. I moaned as my face pushed deeper into the pillow, my back arched painfully, his fingers digging into my hips as he plunged hard and fast from behind. He was rough tonight, but I didn't mind. Leaning forward, Mysterious pressed his chest against my back, his hands reaching around to entwine his fingers with mine. That, paired with the smell of the bar mixed with his musky cologne, did quite a number on my arousal.

"My God, you're wet," he hissed into my ear, tickling my neck.

I squeezed in response, and he groaned, pressing a bit further inside, slowing his pace.

"You gonna cum for me, love?" he asked.

I could feel all of him completely. The deep pulses caused me to grip him like a vice.

"Fuck. So tight, so hot."

God, that voice of his was enough to set me off, but I wanted to ensure we finished simultaneously. I thought I had an even pace, but then he removed one hand from mine and slipped it between my legs. I gasped, my hips rising against his. Tracing his fingers along my entrance, circling himself as well, I nearly lost control. With a flick, he rubbed against me, up and down, sliding around the sides of where we connected and up again to swirl. I moaned, my hands gathering the bedsheet.

"That's it," he whispered.

He quickened, and my mind whirled. Gasping, I couldn't catch my breath as I felt my release quickly approaching.

"Yeah," I whimpered.

"Yeah?" he echoed.

"Yes."

Faster, he pressed on. "Give it to me," he said in a tone that told me he was also about to give in.

"So close," I exhaled sharply. Mysterious may have preferred my silence, but when I gave hints of my release, he edged closer to his own.

One hard thrust sent me over, and I gave a shout, which led him to his release. I closed my eyes, my senses overwhelmed by pure bliss. Mysterious was breathtaking—aggressive yet gentle in demeanor.

Friday night ended with a second round. As he had before, Mysterious remained beside me until I fell asleep, and he disappeared by morning. He made another appearance Saturday night, much to my surprise. Wasn't Liam supposed to be at his sister's?

"Crafty," I whispered as Mysterious pressed his lips against mine.

"Crafty?" He kissed a trail of makeup down my neck.

"Mmmhmm."

"Don't you mean Mysterious?"

"Ah, yes. You're good at that, for sure." Liam was impressive at the game. He played his role a hundred times better than was expected.

"Always."

We switched things up, with me sitting and rocking in his lap. It was nice to bury my face in his neck as he held me—an intimate pose.

"Will I be seeing you again tomorrow?" I asked as he dropped onto the mattress by my side. It seemed our game would become a weekend trend.

"Possibly." His mouth twisted into a gleaming half-grin.

I knew that meant yes, and I giggled, curling toward him as I relaxed. It didn't take long before I fell asleep from the light touch of his fingers tracing lines along my back.

After binge-watching a show on Sunday, I awoke on the couch to Mysterious hovering over me. My yelp made him chuckle, and he took me right there in the dark living room. Hector watched with curious green eyes, and we only simultaneously paused one second to return his stare before we continued with a short laugh.

The first round was fast. Then Mysterious lifted and carried me toward the bedroom, where he held me against the wall, and I wrapped my legs around his waist. We knocked over my nightstand lamp as we migrated to the bed and continued in a vanilla way. It was a delightful thing. He didn't treat me like a porn star each night, a common trend among my past lovers. We'd switch things up and experiment a little, but missionary was never out of the question and became my favorite position, as kissing was my most desired part of the night.

"I'd try for a new record, but…I'm exhausted," Mysterious said with a sigh.

I gave a weak laugh. "I'm thirsty."

"Teach that useless cat of yours to fetch us some water."

We both hummed a small laugh but then lay in silence.

"You know, I never was good at relationships," he muttered.

I gave him a curious look. With a sarcastic laugh, I replied, "Yeah, and my list of relationships has been *amazing*."

"I don't know. It always felt like something was missing. I got tired of the shit."

Liam was rarely so solemn, but I allowed him to continue speaking about his personal life. Besides, perhaps there was a darker side to him that he needed to release.

"Shit, my whole life. Why care about people if they are only going to tear you down? Family, friends, lovers. Fucking hell, it's always about everyone else, and then you get shit on. I stopped caring. I started hating." He exhaled slowly. "Thought I had been successful at barriers. Was dead set on justice and getting revenge on all those who hurt me."

I was surprised. Justice and revenge? Liam had told me all about his past relationships. I knew he had some crappy moments with a few exes, but I would never have thought he would stoop so low into the pits of darkness ever to want revenge. Then, I wondered if this was all simply part of his act.

"But you know what?" he asked, tearing me from my thoughts.

"Hm?" I turned to face him.

"Revenge isn't all that great. Sure, it can feel good for a moment, but what do you do after? It never made me feel any better about the situation. The pain and the hurt…it's still there."

I nodded. "Well, you can't change the past. No matter what."

Mysterious fell into a moment of silence. I had almost dozed off before he spoke again. "I felt like garbage." He stared at the ceiling, unmoving.

I remained fixated on the same spot, understanding. "I felt like a recycled item." From my peripheral, I saw his head turn toward me. He waited for my elaboration. "I was something someone wanted. But once they got their use out of me, they discarded me. I was shaped and molded into something else, something that another wanted. They used me and then threw me away as well. Each time, I change. I become something new, but I'm less like before with every transformation. I will never be who I once was."

We both continued to stare at the ceiling. Silence consumed us.

"Deep," he eventually mumbled.

I hummed in response.

"Can't tell which is worse, to be discarded and never wanted again by anybody else, or to be used like that constantly."

I sighed. "Fuck people."

This time, he grunted in agreeance.

I felt his hand drop by mine, his fingers lightly grazing my skin. I took a deep breath and relaxed. It was another chilly night, but I felt warm beside him. The buzz from the heater lulled me into a light slumber. Mysterious whispered something, but I lost my battle to sleep, and he had left by the time my eyes opened again.

"But I like you, Zoey."

Despite only a few hours of sleep, I awoke energized and ready to work. I only walked through the office door three minutes late, a record for the year.

"Zoey! How's the copy for the holiday section?" Maria chased after me as I wandered to my desk.

"Hm, should be fine. Everybody turned in their stuff on Friday; I only have to finish doing some edits, and then I will look into layouts with Josh and Liam."

"Ugh," Maria sighed. "If Josh shows up to work."

My smirk fell off-kilter. "Hm…yeah, what's up with that? Josh has been missing a lot of work lately, more so than usual."

My boss gave a casual shrug and quickly checked her cell phone. "Some type of flu that's been going around, I suppose. As long as he lets me know ahead of time, it's usually fine, but I won't be pleased if he misses today. We've got to get the standard edition to press by tomorrow night, and then the holiday special is due this weekend."

"Don't worry; I'm sure Liam will get things figured out." Poor Liam always picked up Josh's slack.

Maria eyed her phone again, distracted. "Right, um, well, if you see Josh, send him to my office."

I nodded. I certainly hoped the man wasn't in too much trouble. I heard a familiar, squeaky voice as I headed for my desk. I narrowed my eyes at the rubber duck hovering over the sidewall of my cubicle.

"Zoey needs some coffee!" The toy shook as the voice called out from behind the wall.

I folded my arms. "Quackers…what are you doing here? Aren't you supposed to be with the tech department?"

"I'm on a field trip." The duck was promptly squeezed, giving out a devastating, drawn-out squeal. I bit my lip to suppress a laugh. Quackers was a stress relief device among the tech crew. The rubber duck was squeezed, thrown, and kicked when something went wrong with coding or backups. Slowly, the toy made its rounds across the separate divisions until someone from the tech department arrived to return it to the depths of its torture chamber, where it would receive the brunt of someone's new aggression. I felt a bit bad for Quackers despite it being inanimate.

"Are you getting squeezed due to the deadline crunch?" I asked.

The duck squeaked multiple times again in a quick-fire response. "It seems Josh has called in again," the high-pitched voice called out with a little quack.

"Oh? And is Liam harassing you today?" The duck compressed slowly, the sound screeching for a solid five seconds. My coworkers glared in my direction. "Okay! Okay! Let's go to the break room!" I puffed a sigh and dropped my bag at my desk. "A quick break! I must get back to work on my edits."

Liam's head popped up over the barrier. He grinned and trotted forward, leading the way to the breakroom. I eyed a plateful of donuts and pastries as we entered. Glaring, I debated silently about whether or not I needed one. Liam answered for me, grabbing one of the raspberry cream cheese danishes for himself while shoving another in my hand.

"So, typical Monday for you?" I asked as I took a bite.

Liam eyed the doorway and tossed the duck at a passerby.

"Quackers! You son of a bitch!" The man snatched up the toy and strolled on without acknowledging us.

"Seems like Josh's disappearances are becoming more problematic. I'm not sure how to deal with it. I'll get everything done by the deadline, but it's the principle of it all," Liam exhaled a loud sigh.

"Hopefully, he shows up at some point. Oh, and if he does, send him to Maria's office. She didn't seem pleased, either."

Liam palmed his forehead, groaning. "I hope he's not going to get fired. I mean, he's a decent enough worker, but this is getting a bit out of hand. He deserves to get in trouble, but I also don't want to be left alone working on these holiday projects, and I certainly don't want to be training any new guys during this season."

"May have to buy your own Quackers."

"I'm going to set up a punching bag by my desk. Get in shape while working, eh!" He grabbed his belly and pinched a bit of his skin.

I rolled my eyes. "Shut up, you hyper-metabolic asshole. Go ahead and eat five more donuts while you're at it. It's not like it's going to *your* thighs anytime soon."

He merely smiled and grabbed a second pastry. "So, what're you doing Friday night?"

Ah, there it was, the entire point of luring me into the breakroom.

"I have no plans. Why?"

My heart raced in anticipation.

"Cuz I have tickets for the Grand Gala at the art museum."

My excitement peaked. "What?! How did you get those?"

He straightened into a prideful posture. "I called during one of those radio game shows and actually won. I wasn't really trying, but I knew the answer to their trivia question and gave it a shot."

"Yeah? Well, that's cool!" I caught myself smiling and cleared my throat. "So, I assume you got a *pair* of tickets?"

He nodded. "I was originally going to give them to Josh and his wife, but he's MIA. Besides, I remembered something."

"What's that?" I coyly asked.

"Little Zoey loves the art museum!"

"I do," I confirmed with a large grin. Was Liam going to spoil me by taking me to such an extravagant event?

"So, what do you say? Do you want to get dressed up and go to the gala with me? My car's fixed, so I can pick you up at seven. Fine dining, wine, and dancing."

I feigned deep thought. "Hmm…uh, duh. Yes! I totally want to go!" I hopped on my toes. My face warmed. Liam just asked me on a date, and I was excited about it. I couldn't ignore the butterflies in my stomach and quickly composed myself as I cleaned my glasses on my shirt, giving myself something else to look at besides his attractive face.

"Fantastic! I'll have my suit cleaned! And you, you had better find yourself something nice to wear. I assume you have something."

All the excitement abruptly faded from my expression. My closet was full of t-shirts with pop culture references, plain dress shirts I rarely wore, and a couple of outdated skirts and summer dresses that no longer fit. I had a cute pair of heels I could wear, but other than that, the one formal thing I had was a black and red vintage-style dress that I wore to weddings. It didn't quite seem elegant enough for such a formal event.

"Um, not really, but I think I can scrounge up something."

"No little black dress?" He raised an eyebrow.

I frowned. Oh, there was one of those hanging in the darkest corner of my closet, but it was an impulse buy from years ago when I was thinner and fitter. I had since become a tad bit curvier. The thing stretched and fit like a glove, but was I willing to display my feminine body for all eyes to see at such a prestigious event? Could I lose a few pounds if I stopped eating and worked out daily for the rest of the week? I ground my teeth together at the thought.

"Well, there is one, but I don't think it'll look…appropriate," I said.

"I think you'd look amazing! Seriously, don't go out and buy a new dress for one night. I would feel guilty! Wear whatever you want! Wear what you're wearing now!" He gestured at my body.

I scowled. "If I'm going to a swanky event, you bet your ass I will dress fancy! And…since when do you own a suit?" I quickly changed the subject.

He shrugged. "Everyone should have at least one fine garment in their wardrobe. You never know when such an occasion will arise."

"It's the one from your sister's wedding, isn't it?"

"Yup," he quickly replied.

I laughed. "I'll try on the dress tonight and see how it fits."

"Send me a picture?" He filled his mug with coffee.

"…Maybe."

"Aw, come on! You know I would like it either way!"

Eyeing my stomach, I glared at the donuts and shook my head as I left the room. "Only if I like the way it looks!"

The rest of the day was not as productive as I had planned. I spent most of the time online, switching between tabs as I looked at dresses on various websites. I was thoroughly distracted and slightly stressed about the entire ordeal. Never had I been to an event such as the Grand Gala, and suddenly, all my self-image issues came back to the surface. Would I look good enough in a tight black dress? Should I wear a pantsuit instead? A baggy dress? Was anything formal even baggy? Would wearing something loose make me look fat? Closing the tabs in my browser, I growled. I couldn't do anything about it anyway. Payday wasn't until Friday; it would be too late to purchase a new dress by then. I could use my credit card, but most sites wouldn't deliver the dress on time for the event. There was the possibility of one website I had subscribed to, which had free two-day shipping. I'd have to wait until I got home anyway to measure myself to ensure I ordered the correct size.

"All this stress for no good reason." I dug through my purse, snatching up my medication. My anxiety was through the roof at the thought of dressing up. I always wanted to, but my brain was ruining all the fun. I swallowed the pill and made my way to the bathroom. Anxiety be damned, I wasn't going to let bad memories destroy this opportunity.

"You're not fat. You're not fat." I washed my face in the sink. Most days, I wore little makeup. I never cared much for the stuff unless it was a special occasion, but I felt I needed it more often as I aged. I gaped at my reflection, searching for imperfections—baggy eyes, blemishes, dry skin, flat hair, puffy face, old, and fat.

"You gotta start working out again if you want to remain desirable. It's only going downhill now that you're almost thirty," I grumbled at my reflection.

Since when did I care about being desirable? I didn't want to date. I didn't want a relationship. Because relationships did this to me. They made me second guess myself, and my self-confidence made me worry about my appearance.

I dried my hands, scolding myself. "No, no. He finds you sexy. He mentions it every night he is over. You are not fat and ugly. He is not your ex. He likes your curves, your boobs, your ass." I looked in the mirror once again, turning from side to side. I hadn't worn that little black dress in years. I straightened out my clothes and wiped my fingers along the edges of my smeared eyeliner, hoping to clean it up. Maybe a pushup bra and one of those slimming undergarments would help pull it all together. I took a slow, deep breath.

"If I do full makeup and something with my hair, I can look acceptable for the evening. Black dress and curves—Liam won't be able to resist me," I whispered.

The thought of the evening activities that were sure to follow the gala made me feel better. Nobody else from my past mattered anymore. No bullying and no degrading comments existed anymore. I had left them all behind when I moved to the city.

"Okay. Back to work."

I fluffed my hair and gave myself a once-over before exiting the bathroom and returning to work with nothing more than positive thoughts.

CHAPTER SIX

I scrambled to write my closing on my final article. It was just after five on Friday, and I wanted to leave the office immediately. Preparing for the Grand Gala would take me a while, and I didn't want to spare a minute.

"You finished up?" Liam's voice made me jump.

"Shit! You scared me."

"Hurry it up before Maria comes for us."

I saved my document and quickly closed everything down. Maria rounded the corner before I could ask him what he was worried about.

"Just who I was looking for. You certainly shut down fast today." Our boss casually strolled to my desk, leaning against the cubicle partition.

"Uh, yeah, I've got plans," Liam hesitantly replied.

"Hm, I hate to say this, but you should probably cancel them," Maria boldly stated. I cringed; she was good at cracking the whip but was rarely so harsh about it.

"Cancel?" Liam sputtered. "There's no way. I can't cancel tonight." He eyed me; his expression was one of begging for help.

"Right, we've got an important event to attend tonight," I chimed in.

Maria's eyes widened. "The both of you?"

We nodded.

"A date?" she pried.

"Liam's taking me to the Grand Gala," I explained.

"The Grand Gala?! How on earth did you manage that? Tickets cost around $500 each!" Maria scoffed. "Only the wealthiest in the city get into that Gala. That boy must be in love with you to spend that much!"

"I won them! Radio show!" Liam hollered a bit too loudly.

Maria fell silent for a moment. "I really need you to work, though, Liam. The edition is supposed to go to press first thing Monday morning, and we have last-minute ads that came through."

Liam's face fell into one of irritability, a rare expression. "Why don't you call Josh in, then? He's missed the majority of the week."

"Josh is going through some personal matters right now," Maria snapped.

"Yeah, well, his personal matters are now affecting my life, and I've worked overtime these past two weeks. I may not have paid for these tickets, but this is something Zoey and I have been looking forward to." I nervously held my breath, keeping my mouth clamped shut. Liam rarely showed anger in the workplace, and Maria already seemed on edge.

The older woman held her tight-lipped expression for a moment longer before her face softened. "You know, you're right, Liam. I'm sorry. Josh has certainly gotten away with far more than he should have. I appreciate you picking up his slack. He's supposed to come back to work on Monday. No exceptions this time. But for now, I need someone to get this edition out." Maria suddenly smiled. "Okay, how about this? You guys work tomorrow to finish the publication."

"Both of us? But I've completed all my copy," I protested.

Maria's grin only widened. "I've been trying to get press passes to the Grand Gala for years, and they never allow anyone in for free except for the city's Chronicle newspaper—why never us, I always wonder—and Channel 6 News. This couldn't be any more perfect! Zoey, I want you to take photos of the auction, the dinner, the dance floor, the mayor, and anyone of prestigious standing within our community! Then, tomorrow, you can write a short about the event." My mouth dropped. Was she seriously going to ruin our night with work? "Liam, it should be enough to push our pages up to the next spread. No more canned copy and company house ads. Fill those pages with Zoey's story and make those photos stand out!"

Liam and I exchanged deflated looks.

Maria nodded. "Yes, yes. This edition will be the best of the year!" She noticed our sour expressions. "Well, it's either that or you can stay late tonight. Your choice."

"Yeah…fine," I said. Usually the 'yes ma'am' type, Liam stayed surprisingly quiet.

"Great!" Maria clapped her hands and turned. "Don't look so bitter. You'll both get time and a half tomorrow for your work, and the Grand Gala lasts all night. You'll have plenty of time for dancing and drinking."

Overtime pay did sound good, but it still sucked. However, my spirits lifted. The extra money would cover what I paid for the dress I ended up buying online for the event. Once the door shut behind Maria, Liam slapped his hand harshly against the top of the partition.

"Fucking bullshit!" He loosened his tie, growling.

"Hey, hey…it's okay."

"No, it's not. I don't understand her favoritism with Josh lately, but it's starting to piss me off. And I'm also tired of everything ruining my plans. It's like the universe doesn't want me spending time with you." He took a deep breath, calming himself. I must have held a concerned expression because his face immediately softened. "I'm sorry. I'm just a bit stressed, I guess. I wanted you to have a fun time tonight, not spend it worrying about covering a story for Maria."

"Hey, it's all good! I planned to take pics tonight anyway! I don't care much about the auction, but we can take quick photos and return to the dance floor. I'll gather a few more shots of the highest bidders and their winnings at night's end. And dinner, well, you know how I like to post pics of my food online anyway." I smiled, trying to ease Liam's anger.

"I suppose. Oh! I'll grab a shot of you with the mayor to use in the spread." He stretched out his arms. "The largest photo, full color. Maybe I'll even use it on the cover."

"No," I curtly replied, grabbing my purse. We headed for the exit.

"I'm going to get a photo of you anyway. I bet you'll look stunning. By the way, I never received a pic of you in the little black dress. Did it end up fitting okay?"

I cringed. It fits like a second skin, revealing more of my figure than I thought would be appropriate for the high-class event. "I, uh, actually found something else that I had forgotten about. Something more…elegant." I didn't want him to know I had spent money on our date. It would only make him feel guilty.

Liam grinned; his mood changed. "Well, despite being cockblocked by work tonight, I'm sure it'll be a fine evening."

"Definitely. We won't let this hiccup ruin our night. Besides, we get to drink while on the job."

"Well, when you put it that way!" He walked me to my car. His was parked only a few stalls away, our vehicles the only ones remaining in the parking lot. "Drive safe, Lil Zoey. I'll pick you up at seven."

I could barely contain my excitement. "Okay! See you soon!"

I rushed home, showered, shaved, blow-dried my hair, and was annoyed I got sweaty from the heated steam and dryer. I doused myself in perfume, shimmied into my best set of lingerie, slathered myself in makeup with a smoky eye and glossy pink lips, and slipped on my new dress. Staring at the mirror, I suddenly felt better about myself. In the back of my mind, I heard self-conscious whispers trying to tear away my positive energy. I ignored the thoughts and spread my hands over the flowy black dress. It was a flattering cut for my body shape, accentuating my waist with a spaghetti strap fitted top. It laid loosely about my curvy thighs yet remained tight enough around the hips to highlight my booty. I loved it. It had been a long time since I felt sexy and beautiful in something. I stepped into my black heels and forced silver earrings through my ears. The holes in my lobes were always finicky since I rarely wore jewelry. I picked out a necklace that dripped low enough to rest just above my cleavage.

"You're gonna kill him, Zoey," I whispered, giggling. That was the plan, and I felt I might succeed at keeping him worked up throughout the night.

A knock at the door caused me to jump. I snatched up my silver clutch, slipped on my black leather jacket, which added a touch of my usual style to the ensemble, and opened the door.

"Hi!" Liam beamed from the other side. I held a childish grin and greeted him. "Woah! Zoey! Look at you!"

I held out my arms and couldn't suppress my nervous laugh. "Do I look okay?"

Liam spurted with his lips. "Pfft! You look freaking fantastic! You're going to be the best-looking lady there!"

I giggled and slapped his arm. "Ha! Lady."

He wore a new black suit with matching shined shoes. He clearly had everything washed and pressed for the night. His clean-shaven, square jaw twitched as I looked him over. He looked like a secret agent from an action movie with his hair slicked back.

"Wow, Liam. You're like one of the models in our advertisements."

"I'll take that as a compliment," he grinned widely, his grey eyes glimmering in the dim lighting of the hallway. The smell of his cologne immediately garnered a response between my legs. He was like a damn Pavlov experiment on my sexuality. I took in the scent and sighed.

He hummed as he grabbed my hand. "You ready?"

I nodded and locked the door behind me, letting him lead me down the hall toward the elevator. He guided me to his car and opened the door like a true gentleman. I noticed he had the vehicle cleaned inside and out. It was humorous. At first, I wasn't sure if Liam would treat the event as an actual date, but his actions were unmistakable. He was going to milk the night for all it was worth. I imagined he felt like a child on his birthday with the way he smiled nonstop. Liam finally won by having a date with me. Whereas I would have hated the idea a few weeks ago, now I felt comforted by it. There was no one else I could think of sharing a night like this with. And for a moment, the thought scared me.

Liam took a sharp turn, and something shifted in the back seat. I eyed a black bag that had toppled over, spilling some of its contents—a pair of black leather gloves, a sunglasses case, and a face paint palette. I quickly brought my attention forward, biting back a smile.

"Aw, did my shit spill everywhere?"

"Just a few things." I held back my tongue, wanting to make a joke about his makeup.

"Forgot that was back there."

Liam didn't say much else; the icy drizzle and heavy traffic kept his attention. We arrived just fifteen minutes after the event started. Already, the place was packed. He opened the car door for me again and offered his arm. At the entry, we both made lame remarks about being fashionably late, which the door attendant courteously shared in the forced laughter.

"Oh, wow," I whispered as we entered.

The museum was already an impressive building of marble arches and pillars with a domed ceiling. Dazzling sculptures from what seemed like every era and location worldwide decorated the lobby. Tables lined the edges of the grand hall, covered in black cloths, white roses, and a bottle of champagne each. Liam and I found a small table in the corner that seated three, but luckily, no one bothered to join us. We enjoyed our privacy. Guests occupied the dance floor, holding conversation while sipping their drinks. Extending from the side of the hall was another grand room filled with rows of seats and a large stage where the auction would take place.

"Fancy," Liam said with a nervous sigh as he opened the bottle of champagne at our table. "I wonder what's for dinner."

I grabbed the white sheet with the menu listing. "Caesar salad and shrimp cocktail for starters."

"Dibs on your shrimp," Liam said as he poured me a glass.

"I'll try one; then you can have the rest." I thankfully accepted the drink he offered me. "Choice of Salmon with lemon-pepper butter or the Sirloin with a mushroom feta sauce for dinner served with a side of garlic roasted potatoes, asparagus, and a basket of freshly baked honey wheat bread."

"Ooohhh." Liam loved bread baskets. Actually, who didn't?

"Your choice of chocolate mousse cake, raspberry tart, or a lemon cream cake will follow dinner. Coffee and espresso served by request."

"We are gonna be stuffed by the end of the night."

"Can we just skip to dessert?" I asked as Liam leaned to the side to clink his glass with mine. We sat side by side rather than across from each other. It was more comfortable that way, like how we sat each Friday night at the bar. The champagne was bubbly, not too sweet, but not as sour or bitter as some of the expensive brands I tried. "That's good!"

Liam typed on his cell, searching for the name of the champagne. He whistled. "I would hope so with that price tag." He showed me his phone.

"One hundred and twenty per bottle?" I scoffed. "It's good, but not that good. I'll stick to my giant twelve-dollar bottles, thanks."

"That's why I like you, always a cheap date." Liam winked.

"I'd say. Tonight didn't cost you a single penny!" I laughed.

His face reddened. "Hey, if I could afford it, I would have brought you either way."

"Oh, I'm teasing! I'm grateful you invited me to come along. Thank you."

"I mean, it was between you or…." He cleared his throat.

I eyed him, suddenly feeling a pit in my stomach. Then, I caught his mischievous smile. "One of your dozens of admirers? The girl from the coffee shop? Oh no, wait, Betty from the street corner."

He laughed. "Betty is always my first choice."

We enjoyed the savory flavors of the overpriced food throughout dinner, relishing the fact that it was free. A waiter graciously delivered another bottle of champagne to our table between dishes. We were giggling by desert, the delicacies good enough to be declared moist without either one of us turning up our nose at the word's usage.

"Come on; let's dance." Liam abruptly stood, grabbing my hand. He turned and chuckled, taking my glass from my fingers. "Leave it for a few minutes, you lush! There's plenty more to drink later!"

A live jazz band played something sultry and slow from the corner of the room. I had forgotten that Liam had once been a performer and was adept at dancing, having done a few shows on Broadway when he was younger. He took the lead, guiding me gently back and forth. I wobbled a bit, never having much grace when it came to dancing, let alone in heels.

"You're worried too much about your feet," he said, tapping beneath my chin. "Just look up here and relax."

I hadn't realized I was so tense and gazed at his face, easing slightly. Something about the look in his eyes made me feel shy, something I wasn't used to feeling while around him. His hand lowered from my shoulder, gently sliding down to rest on the small of my back. He carefully pulled me closer to him, and our bodies nearly pressed together. His warmth, scent, and sweet smile finally soothed me. I was no longer nervous but comfortable in his dancing embrace.

"Better?" he whispered.

I nodded. It was strange, but I couldn't remember the last time I danced with a man. My wedding? Even then, that was only a dance or two before my husband had run off to hang out with his groomsmen while I made pleasantries with all of the family. My memories churned over each lover I had since my divorce. Not one man had wanted to woo me in any way. Dating had often resorted to nothing more than a cheap meal and sex at someone's place. There had been no real, lasting effort except for one guy. He was exceedingly kind but not my type. I had given him a chance, but his personality and ambitions were dull. I felt terrible, but I had to fade out of his life slowly. Thankfully, the man had moved on a few months later and found someone equally as monotonous who thought him to be her hero. Good for them.

"You know, no man I've ever known would have dared to take me to a place like this," I mindlessly mumbled.

"Well," Liam started, "you've known some pretty boring people. And some pretty shitty guys."

It was funny. I resented many of my exes because of their blatant use of me for sex. I had been nothing more than eye candy, a body for so many of them. And yet, here I was, keeping myself from having a relationship with Liam by reducing it to nothing more than a sexual relationship. It was confusing. Sure, I wanted sex, but a bit of me wanted more. However, it would be devastating to start a relationship with my best friend, my only friend, to find out that the only reason he had wanted to be with me was because of my body. But then again, he was making an effort tonight, even if the tickets were free. The thoughts further puzzled me, and I lost myself in his warm gaze.

"You deserve things like this, Zoey," he softly stated.

And I felt terrible because Liam deserved this as well, but not with someone like me. I was a mess. There's no way I could live up to his expectations. Liam held me on a pedestal some days, and what worried me the most about getting too close to him was ruining his perception of me.

He brushed a strand of hair from my eyes, resting his palm against my face. And I found that I wanted him closer, but I argued with myself. That would only complicate things. What would happen if he kissed me? Everything would feel weird the rest of the night, the rest of my career. I overthought everything as I usually did.

As Liam leaned in close, the song faded into silence, and a voice called out over the speakers. "Ladies and gentlemen, the auction will be starting in five minutes. Those who would like to bid, please take your seats in the east wing."

I quickly pulled away from Liam. "Shit, I got to take photos."

Liam released me, averting his gaze. "Yeah, yeah. Of course."

I rushed to the table, grabbing my clutch beneath my jacket to find my phone. I sauntered past him into the east wing, snapping pictures of some sculptures and art along the way without much thought. We just needed the visuals for the article. I approached the main stage and spoke with someone about emailing the final bid results. It didn't take much convincing from the museum proprietor to agree. I sat in the second row, where I could gather a few photos of the items for sale and the auctioneer. Liam sat next to me, two champagne glasses in his hands.

"Ah, you came prepared," I said as I took pics with my phone.

It was to my luck that the mayor spoke after the welcoming speech. I snagged a few shots of him and then spent the next hour murmuring to Liam about the bidders and artwork for sale. One particular item was a white canvas with a smear of olive green and various browns. It was hideous.

Liam leaned to the side, whispering in my ear. "And next is 'Baby Poop-Splosion' by artist Ireal E. Stink."

I snorted. "Wanna bet that goes for over one hundred thousand?"

Liam peered over his shoulder, eying the bidders as they lifted their signs while each number soared higher and higher. "See that man with the white mustache? His wife keeps elbowing him. I'm guessing she's having an affair with that artist, or maybe she's a major shareholder in the top-brand toilet paper industry."

The auctioneer smacked his hammer. "Sold! For one hundred and twenty-two thousand."

Liam's mouth dropped as he gave a dramatic gasp. "One hundred and twenty-poo thousand!" I slapped his arm and quickly stood, taking a picture of the ugly painting as I passed. I had enough of the uppity atmosphere.

"You're so immature." I rolled my eyes. His jokes may have been awful, but they still made me laugh.

We spent the rest of the evening drinking, dancing, and chatting at our table. We took selfies and made silly faces, posting the content to our social media pages. Before I knew it, the end of the event had arrived. It was eleven o'clock, and most of the attendants had already left. Liam guided me to the exit as I giggled and drank the last bit of my champagne; a man in a black suit and tie with a silver platter quickly snatched it from my hand.

"Have a good evening, miss," he curtly added as he dashed toward the back.

"Hey! One second; stand over here." Liam ushered me in front of a marble sculpture of a woman in flowing drapery holding a seductive pose. He waved his hand. "More to the right. Get in there." He lifted his phone.

I looked over my shoulder and mimicked the woman's posture. Liam took several pictures as I shuffled and pulled off different stances and expressions.

"Okay, okay! We gotta go!" I shouted.

"One more! One more! It takes a few shots to capture a masterpiece," Liam demanded.

By this time, we were the last attendants in the building.

"Hurry! We're gonna get in trouble!"

He took one more and then rushed to my side, grabbing my hand as we exited, the remaining staff wishing us a good night. As expected, Liam used every last minute to be with me. I didn't mind. I loved it all.

"That was fun," he said. "Did you have a good time?"

I beamed with delight. "Yeah. I did. Thank you."

"We should do it again sometime." He opened the car door for me and then entered from his side. "Well, somewhere more accommodating to my wallet."

"We can always come back to check out the displays. Or…there's the zoo!" I suggested.

"The boardwalk sometimes has live bands and food trucks. When it warms up, we should check those out."

"Definitely."

We conversed on the way to my apartment about various events we could attend, restaurants we had to try out, and movies we should see. I didn't think much of it. I needed to get out more, and with Liam, I could trust him enough for a night of fun. However, butterflies hit my stomach as he pulled up to my complex. Would he follow me upstairs? Was he expecting something from me at this point?

"Well, Zoey. Thank you for coming with me tonight. I suppose I should let you get some rest. We both have work in the morning."

My giddiness dissipated. I had forgotten. Maria ruined everything. "Um, yeah. I drank quite a bit, so I better hydrate and get things ready for the morning."

Liam's expression turned somber. "Same."

We sat awkwardly in silence for a moment. My eyes drifted to the dashboard clock—11:45 pm. I sighed and reached for the door handle. As I began to turn in my seat, Liam suddenly grabbed me, guiding my face towards his. I inhaled sharply as his lips pressed against mine. It only lasted a second before he pulled away, leaving me stunned.

"I'm sorry," he whispered, his lips still close to mine. "I just knew I would regret it if I didn't."

I opened my eyes, seeing his smoldering in the light of the streetlamps. He looked serious, his teeth grazing his lower lip for a change. It was a sultry expression that I wouldn't deny looked sexy. Damn it all. I leaned forward and kissed him back, my hands traveling up his body to his hair. He moaned, shuddering against me as his tongue slipped past my lips. He tasted like sweet champagne; I only wanted to savor more of him. Without thinking, I slipped my hand between his legs, feeling the heat and growth that had developed there.

"Oh, Zoey," he groaned, spreading his legs, wanting more. But his mentioning of my name snapped me alert. This went against our game. We were supposed to keep our personal lives out of the sexual fun. I sat back in my seat, clearing my throat and smirking. He looked surprised, his eyes wide and mouth gaping as he caught his breath.

"That'll give you something to think about tonight," I whispered, kissing him on the cheek. How badly I wanted him. I desired to say, 'screw it all,' and pull him upstairs to my bedroom, but I didn't want to ruin our lovely game.

"You're gonna kill me," he rasped.

I snickered in response and opened the car door, slipping out. "I'll see you in the morning."

"Yeah, right, the morning." He swallowed hard.

"By the way," I started, "you look excellent in a suit." I winked and shut the door.

Liam's smirk shined in the pale light, visible even through his car's tinted windows. He waited until I entered my building to leave. I was a bit disappointed. Working in the morning ruined the rest of our night, and I was surprised at how much I enjoyed the date. I would have loved to have gone to a late-night coffee shop with Liam. Invite him up to my room. Go back to his place. But perhaps it was for the best. I didn't want to jump into what he would perceive as a relationship immediately. No, it was best to keep the romance separate from our friendship for now.

"Hey, Hector! Did you miss me?" I asked as I entered my apartment. Hector meowed at me angrily and headed straight for his food. "No, but you missed your food, I see." I dumped a little scoop into his bowl and called him fat. He had to have mini-meals throughout the day as he could not be trusted with a full bowl to last him.

I went to the bathroom, undressed, washed off my makeup, and brushed my teeth. I debated a bit about showering and decided a quick one now was better than getting up earlier in the morning to deal with it. After a quick wash, I grabbed a glass of water, swallowed a pill to prevent a later headache, and slipped into bed. Exhaustion hit faster than expected. I plugged in my phone, clearing my notifications—nothing too important, just hearts and likes on my photos from the evening. I curled up with my softest blanket and called Hector, wanting him to lay beside me. Before I felt him jump on the bed, I had fallen fast asleep.

My rest only lasted for a short while as something awoke me. It was a strange feeling, nearly ominous. The room seemed darker than usual, colder. I looked toward my bedroom window and gasped. A figure blocked out the light.

"God! You scared the shit out of me." I exhaled a nervous laugh as I sat up in bed. The scent of cologne reached my nostrils, and I relaxed.

"Did you have fun tonight?" Mysterious asked, his tone slightly on edge.

"Yeah, of course I did," I spoke quietly, unsure how to respond as we weren't meant to talk about our regular lives while playing the game.

"I don't like you seeing other people," he said.

"Oh, it was just some…work function. No big deal."

"It looked like a big deal, the way you dressed. The way you kissed him."

I smirked. "Oh, is someone jealous?"

Mysterious approached the bed, grabbing my wrists in one hand. It hurt slightly. He usually wasn't so rough. "You're mine, love. No one else's."

Before I could respond, his lips were against mine, rough and forceful. I could barely breathe. His free hand gripped my breast through my t-shirt, massaging me. After his tongue invaded my mouth and his hand dipped lower into my panties, he released my lips only for a moment to push me back onto the bed and climb over me. I gasped for air just before he kissed me again. He was ravenous, warm, hard—extremely hard. I moaned as his finger slipped inside me without resistance. I was soaking wet, ready for him.

"Tell me you're mine," he hissed.

I groaned, already feeling myself near the edge.

"Tell me," he insisted.

"I'm yours."

"Again." He pressed his thumb against the nub above my entrance, his finger curling inside me.

I screamed, "I'm yours!"

"Only mine," he stated, quickening his pace.

"Oh, God! Only…only yours. Yours!" My fingers twisted the blankets beneath me.

"Don't fight it. Give it to me. I'm having you all night."

"All night? But, but I have work—ah!"

He was so forceful, so demanding.

"Come on, love. That's it." Faster and faster, he played with me, his white eyes locked on mine. I screamed, and he didn't let up as I came hard, squeezing his fingers as I rocked my hips against his hand. His mouth covered my shouts, his fingers continuing with their quick pace. He wasn't going to stop. I wrapped my legs around his waist, craving more.

"Do you want me?" he asked.

His warm kisses moved to my neck.

"Yes, I want you."

"How badly do you want me?" He raised my shirt with a feral need, his mouth crushing against my nipple. His ministrations below slowed, his fingers lightly teasing my entrance, keeping my arousal peaked.

"Bad," I huffed.

"Keep telling me," his words vibrated against my skin as he lowered. "Don't stop talking."

I gasped as he licked where his fingers had been, slicking the folds and tasting me. My hands went to his head, gripping the hood of his black sweater. I mumbled about how badly I wanted him, needed him. Satisfied hums vibrated against me, making me all the more stimulated. Soon, my words turned into nothing more than cries and moans. I tried to fight against his hold on my thighs. It was too much. I could barely catch my breath. Just as I was about to release a second time, he removed his mouth and softly exhaled, his breath tickling me. My legs quaked against his hold. Slowly, his lips lightly pecked my folds—soft, light butterfly kisses that drove me mad. His mouth trailed upward, over my abdomen to my chest. The sound of his lowering pants zipper rang out in the air, and one of his large hands reached underneath me, raising my hips. I felt the twitch of his tip against me. He was hard, hot, already slick with his juices. How I wanted to touch him, taste him. I lowered my hand to grab him, but he again locked my hands over my head.

"You're mine tonight. I get to do whatever I want to you."

I didn't protest. When Mysterious took complete control, it was sexy as hell. He teased me with just the edge of his twitching member, circling me as he kissed me. The light touches turned me on more than complete contact. Being teased was fun. How he managed to keep me soaking wet was mind-blowing. No one had ever had this power over me. I would let him do anything to me. Well, almost anything. Mysterious sank inside me just a half-inch, pulsing a few times before he pulled out and repeated the action, slowly pressing further each time. It drove me wild.

His teeth grazed the base of my neck and collarbone, making me shiver. "Please," I whispered.

"Please, what?" he growled against my flesh.

"Please put it inside. All of you. I want to feel all of you."

He retracted completely, raising his head to gape at me, his lips slightly parted. It was a cocky look, and I loved it.

"All of me?"

I nodded.

His teeth ground together as he thrust deep inside, wholly. I shouted. He pressed against my furthest walls. It ached slightly, like pressing against a bruise, but felt amazing simultaneously. He hissed with pleasure and pulled back, pushing hard into me again. As his hips smashed against mine, my entire body jolted against the mattress, my breasts bouncing with each impact. Small groans of pleasure escaped him as he greedily gazed upon me with his lustful eyes. One after another, pound for pound, I edged closer to another orgasm. His expression, I couldn't tear my sight away, was incredibly erotic. He commanded me, dominated me, and did so without words. His hands gripped my hip tightly while the other moved to my lower abdomen, pressing down. It made me tighter against him, aching for release. I cried out, rocking at an uneven pace against him, desperate to reach my peak. Mysterious' eyes narrowed, and I could see, along with feeling it, that he was about to blow at any moment. He growled, his strong jaw trembling as he fought his pleasure.

"Give it to me," I whispered.

His attention diverted to my words for a moment, distracting him. "You get no say in this, love."

My breaths grew faster. "Please, give it to me. I want to feel it." He remained quiet, and I knew he was losing his resolve. He wasn't as tough as he liked to pretend to be. I tried to give him my sexiest expression, though it didn't take much as my lustful state completely overtook me. "I'm so close. Cum with me."

His throat moved as he swallowed thickly.

"Yeah, I know you want it, baby," I hissed, grinding shamelessly against him.

"Cum," he demanded. "Now."

His voice, eyes, face paint, and tight grip were enough to send me to the brink. He was losing control, and even that was sexy. I listened to his grunts, how they quickened with each thrust. We matched an even pace with our panting, and soon, I felt the edge of release hanging by a thread.

"Almost, almost!" my voice raised in pitch.

We soaked each other, and I screamed after a couple more slams, grinding against him with intense pleasure. A quick shout slipped past his lips as he joined me in his orgasm, and we came together. An incredible heat filled me as he vibrated with each burst of his climax. My hands cupped his face, and he leaned down to kiss me, his thumb reaching between us to roll against my bud above his quaking cock. I moaned against his lips as my peak rose to a second stage. I had never felt so hot before. I craved more, never wanting him to stop.

Mysterious continued with his game, not relenting against me until I came two more times and he another. It was the best sex of my entire life.

I don't remember falling asleep. But there was one point when I felt the bed shift and heard the front door close. I eyed my phone. It was three in the morning. I was going to be exhausted at work.

"Worth it," I whispered as I closed my eyes and fell asleep in a near-instant.

I dreamt of Mysterious' words echoing in my mind.

"You're mine. No one else's."

CHAPTER SEVEN

I awoke the following day groggy, my lower abdomen sore, and my legs weak. Groaning, I rolled across the mattress to pick up my phone. I was *incredibly* tempted to sleep in another hour, but I knew Liam would be waiting for me at the office. I didn't even care to shower again after the night's events. Liam would have to deal with the smell of sex if he ventured too close. The idea made my nose wrinkle, and I dabbed perfume across my body. As I readied the coffee maker, I debated showering again, feeling gross by the idea of wallowing in my filth all day, but I didn't have the time; I had already slept an extra half hour.

"Ugh!" I snarled, feeling the morning grumps settling in. "Let's just get today over with."

Hastily, I tossed cat food into Hector's bowl, some of the tiny nuggets bouncing and scattering onto the floor. I threw on my coat, filled my thermos halfway with ice to cool the hot brew, and chugged most of the drink before I got into my car. It was freezing out, the ground covered in a thin sheet of ice from the previous night's drizzle. As my car warmed up, I shivered and growled miserably, my teeth clattering. It was Saturday morning. I was supposed to be in my warm bed with my fluffy cat.

"Stupid Maria…" I huffed as I slammed the car into reverse and rushed to the office.

Traffic was slow that morning, and when I arrived, Liam's car was in the parking lot. I tapped the brakes as I parked, the ice threatening to pull my vehicle sideways. I hated the cold. And though it technically wasn't winter yet, it may as well have been, which was even more dreadful as I loved autumn, but it seemed mother nature skipped right over it. I stomped into the office, slammed my timecard into the noisy, old machine with a clunk, and tossed my bag onto my desk as I entered my cubicle.

It took only a few minutes before I heard a lazy scuffle from down the hall past the breakroom. I leaned out of my small office and watched Liam move with a lethargy matching mine. He yawned and rubbed his unkempt hair. It looked like he cared about appearances as much as I did today. Stubble lined his jaw. It was cute. I quickly shook the thought away as his gaze met mine. His sleepy demeanor perked only a bit, his eyes remaining heavy. It seemed he wanted to be excited but couldn't muster the full enthusiasm.

"Hey," he mumbled.

I moved toward the break room with him. "Hey."

"Slept like shit," Liam groaned. "Too much champagne, maybe."

"Yeah, same," I said with an exhale.

I stood in the corner, finishing the coffee in my thermos, watching the man prepare a pot. He wore casual clothing, not caring about the office dress code as it was the weekend. It was honestly the most casually dressed I had ever seen him—sweatpants and a t-shirt with a superhero logo on the chest. It made me want to curl up with him the rest of the morning. Various thoughts of affection flooded my mind, and I had to clear my throat to interrupt the silence.

"Worth it, though," Liam sleepily stated.

"Hm?"

"Last night and being tired today. I have no complaints."

"Oh. Yeah!" I said with a quiet laugh, wondering why I felt so anxious around him.

Liam turned toward me as the coffee sputtered its hot water. He leaned against the counter, a faint smirk on his face. "Though I am sad the night ended so soon."

"Hm, but it was still a good night. And there was plenty to think about when I went to bed."

Liam softly bit his lip, his hand lightly scratching his chest. "Uh, yeah. There was." He shuffled a little, and my eyes caught a glimpse of his erection forming in his sweatpants. "That kiss, though…."

My heart began to race. I had forgotten we kissed in the car as he dropped me off at my apartment. I had so desperately wanted to have more of him. I had even touched him in ways that I never had outside my bedroom. The memory made my chest heavy, my breaths quickening.

"It caught me by surprise," I admitted.

"But…it wasn't bad, was it?" He eyed me nervously.

We shouldn't have been talking about it. Even though it happened outside our bedroom personas, I didn't want to get too caught up in the flirtatious talk at work. I wasn't sure if I could hold back, especially after seeing Liam aroused.

My body betrayed me. I moved closer to him, my hands grazing his as I reached for a mug. "Oh, it wasn't so bad," I playfully spoke as I poured the hot brew. I leaned across him, dangerously close, and shook a sugar packet into the black drink.

"Oh? Not *so* bad, eh?" He played back, his eyes smoldering.

I chewed on my lip this time as his demeanor dropped to a more intense nature.

I grinned and stirred the coffee. "It was all right." I handed the mug to him after prepping it just as he liked.

Liam lightly grasped it, his fingers over mine. He leaned in close, his mouth by my ear. "Perhaps I should try again, then?"

I froze. No, I didn't want this. My gaze met his. He smelled like old Liam without the cologne, but I could detect the trace scent of his shampoo. His lips remained slightly parted, his tongue lightly tracing them. I swallowed hard. I did want it. I enjoyed the attention; I desired the flirting; I wanted his kiss. He gently placed the mug onto the counter at his side, and he gripped my hips, quickly spinning me to trade places. Before I could make a sound, his lips were upon mine.

A light gasp interrupted the intense silence, and I wasn't sure if it came from me, him, or both of us. But I reached for him, my fingers clawing at his t-shirt, pulling him closer. He lifted me as his tongue darted into my mouth, setting me on the counter and pressing between my legs. A moan slipped through my throat as his fingers tangled with my hair while my hands felt his warm body heat through his clothing. He was just the right height where I could feel the edge of his erection against me, between my legs, and I reached low, tracing the tip sticking out from the top of his sweatpants underneath his shirt. My god, he was so sexy. How had I not realized it before?

I slightly lifted his shirt, my thumb slipping over his swelling head. He wasn't as wet as usual, but I felt some light lubrication after a few nudges. He twitched and hissed against my lips. I tugged on his waistband, readying to dip my hand deep inside, when a noise came from the doorway.

"Ahem!"

We both gasped and abruptly pulled apart. I hopped off the counter as Liam adjusted himself, grabbing the coffee mug and holding it below his waist. Dread washed over me as I stared straight into Maria's glaring eyes. This was it; I was going to get fired for sure. And Liam, too. I just knew it.

"Well…good morning," she shortly stated, her eyes peering back and forth at us.

I had no words, and neither did Liam. I could sense his desire to die on the spot just as much as mine. For a moment, no one spoke. Maria looked off to the side, glanced at her phone, and then eyed me again with her frosty stare.

"Zoey, a word. Liam, get to work," she said.

"Yes, ma'am," Liam stated as he briskly moved away. Maria slipped to the side to allow his exit.

She motioned me to follow her, and I quickly did just that. We strolled to the front of the workplace toward the entrance. Instead of meeting in her office as expected, she left the building. I wanted to apologize and make a thousand excuses, but nothing sounded good in my head, and I was too damn afraid to speak up. Maria had a feisty temper, and I couldn't foresee any of my words helping the situation.

"The coffee in the breakroom is awful. Let's get something good across the street," she muttered.

I swallowed and trailed behind like a kicked puppy. The coffee shop was nearly empty. It seemed nobody wanted to venture out in the dreadful, icy weather this Saturday morning. Maria ordered her usual with an extra shot of espresso. She turned toward me.

"Order something," she demanded.

I didn't want anything. I had already drunk my morning coffee, and I wasn't hungry. Instead, I felt I was on the verge of vomiting. Still, I didn't want to make things more awkward by refusing.

"Uh…pumpkin…spice." I don't know why I ordered it, but it was the first thing I saw. And it was no lie; those drinks were tasty as hell. The sugar would destroy my nerves further, but I figured I might as well go all-in if I were to have a panic attack later.

Quickly, the baristas made the drinks, but it felt like an eternity to me. The tension was so high; I think the café employees sensed it. They called out the order, and Maria quickly snagged the two drinks and approached a table in the far corner of the room where we could have some privacy from prying ears.

"So…did you get the photos last night?" she asked as she sat.

"Yes," I meekly replied.

"And the story?"

"I…will…I still need to write it. I was going to write it first thing this morning."

Maria hesitated. "After you finished making out with Liam?"

I cringed. "I'm…I'm sorry. It's seriously the first time anything like that has happened. We both got carried away. We're tired; it was a late night. I dunno what to say." I quickly shut up, not wanting to ramble further.

"I didn't realize you two were dating."

"We aren't!" I sputtered a bit too loud.

Maria blew on her coffee. She barely looked me in the eye as she spoke, but her mannerisms were terrifying enough. She was a larger woman, and her thick winter coat, scarf, and fluffy hair made her look more intimidating. "So…this is a new thing?"

"I-I…I guess so." I stared blankly at the table, wondering when her wrath would finally come down upon me. "I don't even know what we are."

Maria scoffed and then snorted a laugh. "Huh…yeah. I know what that's like."

I finally took a deep breath, the first I remembered since she caught Liam and me in the breakroom. "Huh?"

"Listen, Zoey; I'm not going to fire you for kissing Liam while at work so you can relax."

Her tone and demeanor finally softened, and I suddenly felt a tremendous weight lift from my chest.

"Besides," she muttered, eyeing the café. "It would be hypocritical of me."

Now, I was intrigued. "Hypocritical?"

"We don't necessarily have a policy against dating within the office. Coworkers or…employees alike."

Did I understand her correctly? Was she insinuating something? I gave her a questioning look, and her tenacity crumbled.

"God, I have to tell someone, and I have no idea why I am telling you, but after seeing you and Liam, I figured now was the best time to get this shit off my chest." Maria sipped her coffee and exhaled sharply. She seemed more nervous than I did.

"What's going on?" I asked, still not touching my drink.

"It's Josh."

"…Josh?"

"Yeah. Josh and I…we…."

She didn't need to say more. I understood completely.

"But he's married…." I started.

"Getting divorced," Maria quickly interjected.

I was stunned. Josh and his wife seemed to have the perfect marriage. They appeared happy, talked throughout the day, and had lunches together. It made no sense to me why they would get a divorce. "Wow…I guess fairytales really don't exist." Honestly, I was disappointed. Seeing Josh's admiration for his wife and family was sometimes inspiring. He gave me hope for a better future.

Maria shrugged. "It's a part of life. You marry young, make mistakes, and try to fix them, but you know, deep down, that spark isn't there anymore. You're only lying to yourself at that point, wasting everybody's time." I listened carefully to Maria's words. "They're still friendly, thankfully."

I nodded slowly. "So, the divorce…was it because of…."

"Me?" she laughed. "No! No. But I can't say there wasn't a bit of flirting beforehand. We never really continued with anything or got involved. They simply…grew apart." She sipped her coffee, closed her eyes, and heaved another loud sigh. "I found him one morning at his desk long before opening time. He had slept in the office. We started talking, and…one thing led to another," she explained.

"So, is that why he's been missing so much work?" I asked.

Maria nodded.

"And is that why you constantly stare at your phone and make excuses for him?" It was a bit bold of me to say, but she did owe an explanation for the favoritism she had been playing lately.

"Yes. I can't help it. I want to make sure he gets through this okay. I know I haven't been fair to Liam or you. I shouldn't have messed with your date last night. Josh has been struggling with this, and I've been trying to give him time and space to adjust. It's selfish, I know." Maria looked ashamed, and I suddenly felt terrible for her. She was infatuated with Josh, and it was fogging her mind about how to deal with him professionally.

"Do you…love him?" I asked.

Maria's mouth flipped into a frown. "I…well…I wouldn't say that. I mean…we are close. We've…." Her face reddened.

"You've done things?" I asked with a grin.

"Of course we have! In my office, in his car, at my place! What do you want from me?" she huffed. "I shouldn't have said anything."

I laughed.

"Don't you laugh! What about you and Liam, hm?"

My face fell. "What about us?"

"Well, do you love him? Have you done things?"

My heart stopped. "Love? Ha, no. I mean, I care about him a lot. But love…that's just silly."

Maria rolled her eyes. "Aw, come on. How long has it been? You've been up each other's asses practically since the day you met! What kind of things have you done?"

I wanted to hide. Why was Maria suddenly playing the part of my best friend? I suddenly realized that I had closed myself off from society so much that I didn't have any close female friends here in the city. I had no one to talk to but Liam. In fact, I spoke to Maria the most out of everyone in the office besides him. I looked her over. She was overworked, divorced years ago, and never had kids. Was she my future? She had no one else either, having devoted the entirety of her life to her business. I suddenly felt sad for her. No wonder Maria clung to Josh. He was probably all she had and the most she had in years.

"Okay, so we play this game," I gave in.

Maria's eyes lit up. "Oh? Kinky stuff?"

"Kind of."

"BDSM?" she questioned. I was surprised she even knew what that was.

"Not too kinky. Just…fun."

"Role-playing?" she followed up.

"We…." I held my breath as I thought for a moment. Well, I guess one could call it that. I didn't know how to respond, but my silence was evidence enough.

Maria cackled, her eyes creasing. It was a rare expression for her. "Ah, to be young again! I always thought you two would be cute."

"Maria…why are we here discussing these things?"

Her laughter died down, and she stared at her hands as they clasped around the coffee cup. "I can't answer that myself. Perhaps I need…hmm…validation."

"Validation?"

"Am I doing something wrong?" she asked. Worry filled her eyes, yet another foreign expression to her usually cold demeanor.

"With Josh?"

She nodded.

I smiled. Poor Maria was in love, and it was confusing the hell out of her. "Listen. As long as you two aren't hurting anybody else, screw what people think."

Maria's appearance immediately brightened.

"I mean…you have been a bit unfair to Liam, but other than that, if Josh makes you happy, then why would that be wrong?"

"I will apologize to Liam. I'll take him to lunch or give him a gift card to that bar you guys like to go to every Friday night."

"He'd like that." I nodded.

"But being Josh's boss…."

"Just don't play favorites within the company at the expense of others. Put your foot down and draw a clear line of boundaries. At home, everything's love and sex. At work, Josh has to behave." Maria bobbed her head slowly as I spoke. "And I will keep that in mind with Liam as well."

She cackled again. "Yes! We both will have to behave ourselves, right?"

I let out a slow breath, feeling more at ease with the situation.

"Even though those tasty morsels are hard to resist," she added with a snicker.

"Maria!" I couldn't help but laugh. Josh was not attractive in my eyes, but I suppose to each their own.

"Okay, kid, let's get back to work." Maria stood. I followed her actions. "Oh, and Zoey…."

"Yeah?" I asked as I tightened the scarf around my neck.

"Can we both keep this a secret? Until…I'm ready?"

I giggled. "Uh, yeah. Definitely."

Maria led the way, and the rest of the walk to the office consisted of banter about the horrid weather. I drafted my article as fast as possible while Liam stayed on his side of the building doing the graphics work. I felt guilty. He had far more work to do than I did, and he would still be there at least another hour or two after me. As I clocked out, I messaged him goodbye. I didn't hear from him for at least half an hour after leaving.

'I'll see ya later,' was all he sent.

'Okay.' I smiled, wondering if Mysterious would make a scheduled appearance that night.

As soon as I arrived home, I crashed into my bed. Hector immediately followed, chirping in his merry way. Oh, he loved snuggle time. I didn't want to sleep and throw off my schedule, but once the black furry baby curled up against me and started purring, I was out within minutes.

I awoke much later. A strange rosy hue overtook my apartment with an ultra-vibrant sunset, and I yawned and stretched, waking Hector. He did the same and then squeaked, pawing at my face.

"Are you hungry, bubba?"

"Me-ow!"

"Oh? That hungry?"

"Meow."

"Starving?"

"Moww." A quieter half-purr, half-meow, came from his tiny pink mouth.

"Okayyyy," I groaned as I rolled out of bed.

Hector leaped from the mattress ahead of me, his tail perky and in a straight line. He led me to his bowl, mewing all the way. I dropped the crunchies into his dish and opened my refrigerator door. Hunger caused my belly to growl, but nothing sounded good. I eyed the aged produce in my bottom drawer. The soft cucumber and wilted lettuce didn't look that appealing. I dug out some cheese and pepperoni and used my last tortilla to make myself a pizza wrap. With my snack prepared, I plopped onto the couch to watch movies.

It felt far too long since I had a night of relaxation with my cat. Fat and happy, he immediately joined me on the sofa and curled into a ball, falling fast asleep. After a couple of films, I noticed my phone flashing. I had missed a call and a text message from my mother. I frowned. The woman barely talked to me unless she wanted something.

'Are you coming home for Thanksgiving?'

I groaned. I had nearly forgotten the holiday was coming up on Thursday. The special edition would go out early on Monday so everyone could have off for the holiday and the rest of the weekend.

'I dunno,' I texted her back.

'I want you to meet Carl.'

I rolled my eyes. Carl. He was her latest boyfriend.

'I have a lot of work to do,' I quickly messaged back.

'You haven't been home in over a year.'

'I don't like coming home.'

'You know, your family misses you!'

"I highly doubt that," I muttered under my breath.

'I don't want to play twenty questions with everyone. Just tell them I'm still single, I'm not pregnant, I'm never moving back, and I'm not getting back together with Mason.'

'Well, I want to see you. I have Christmas presents for you.'

'I don't have much money to come home.' It was a partial truth.

'Carl will give you some money. He wants to meet you.'

Of course, Carl would be the one to give me money to 'help out.' I assumed my mother thought he had lots of money, like all her previous boyfriends.

'I'm not taking Carl's money,' I wrote.

'Just come home.'

I growled. I hated that place. I disliked nearly everyone there. I did not want to return to that shithole town.

'I miss you.' Another message popped up.

"God, you're trying *really* hard." I scowled at the phone. All I wanted to do was spend that weekend in bed with Liam. My thoughts surprised me. I didn't think of Mysterious but imagined Liam. This was getting out of hand. Maybe a weekend away would be good for me.

Begrudgingly, I texted back. *Fine. I'll come. But I don't want to see a bunch of people.'*

'When are you coming down?'

Despite the edition going out early, I still had to work Monday through Wednesday for next week's copy. *I'll drive down Thursday.'*

'Okay, we'll have our own little Thanksgiving on Friday then. And then we are supposed to meet with Grandma and the others on Saturday.'

I sighed harshly. I did not want to see my family. Why should I be tormented on the holidays?

'Okay. Then I'm coming home on Sunday,' I replied.

'Okay. Love you.'

I hesitated, feeling an immense amount of irritation rising in the pit of my stomach. *Love you.'* I texted back.

With a heavy sigh, I tossed my phone to the edge of the couch and laid back, covering my face. Hector meowed. I eyed him, realizing I had forgotten I would need someone to care for him while I was gone. I grabbed my phone and promptly messaged Liam.

'Hey, you gonna be in town for Thanksgiving?'

I waited a minute before he responded. *'As far as I know. I will go to my parents' house this weekend, but it's only an hour away. Why?'*

'Mom's making me come home.'

'Ew.'

I laughed. Liam knew all about my family situation. *'Can you please come over and feed Hector while I'm gone? I usually give him small meals throughout the day, but you don't have to do that. At least once a day.'*

'Sure. No problem.'

'You can even chill with him for a while if you want. I don't care. I just need him to be fat while I'm gone.'

'Oh, we're totally gonna have a sleepover.'

'Just don't let in any strays.'

'Party pooper.'

We chatted a bit about work and Maria. I held back on telling him about the Josh situation. I didn't want to betray Maria's trust immediately, even though I knew Liam would keep it a secret. I moved toward the bedroom. I was tired of movies; I could play games on my phone until I fell asleep.

'So, about Codename: Mystery.' His message popped up.

I smirked. *'What about it?'*

'I'm sad that you'll be gone over the weekend. I was planning on taking advantage of the holiday vacation.'

"Damnit," I cursed aloud.

'Well…I could cancel plans,' I typed with a grin.

'Ohhhh…that could be tempting. Have our own slumber party?'

I chewed my lip. *'Oh, yes. Very tempting.'*

'You'd never hear the end of it,' he replied.

'Ugh…I'm already a bad daughter, remember?'

'When you get back. Wink, wink.'

'Duh. Absolutely.'

I walked to the bathroom to get ready for bed. As soon as I exited, a body crashed into me. I was pressed against the wall, Mysterious' lips crushing mine.

"I've been thinking about you all day," he said in his husky British tone.

I had to admit. I missed Liam's voice but didn't want to ruin the façade.

"Yeah? Miss me?"

"Every minute that my body isn't pressed to yours," he rasped as he kissed me again, his hands all over my body. I groaned, reminded of how hot everything had gotten in the breakroom earlier that morning.

"I feel the same way," I replied between the aggressive kisses.

I removed my shirt and quickly pulled him toward the bed, feeling the need to have control for once. He fought back, and I laughed.

"Bold thing tonight," he said.

"Let me have you," I whispered, lowering on the bed while he remained standing. I gripped his pants, which he eagerly unzipped, readying himself for me.

"Usually, I like being in control," he murmured.

"Mmm, but you can still be. Just let me pleasure you a bit for a change."

I removed him from his pants. He was still slightly flaccid, but he quickly hardened once I pressed my lips to his tip. I tasted him, my tongue rolling over the soft pink flesh. He lightly hissed, his hand immediately gripping my hair. I had to admit that I wasn't the best at oral or the most experienced. But with him, something made me want to suck him dry—lust, hormones, desire. I even shocked myself. I enjoyed it.

"Fuck, that's good," he whispered, shoving himself deeper into my mouth.

I gagged. That was something new. I usually didn't like the overly pornographic type of sex, but I wanted to please him. I willed myself to relax, focusing on him.

Mysterious held onto my hair, thrusting his hips forward as I swallowed him nearly whole. After a couple of times gagging, I put my hand in front of my mouth, giving myself some relief. I pulled away, using my hand to massage his shaft, my tongue flicking over the slit of his head. He twitched, gasping at the sensation. I wanted him to cum for me this way. I wanted him to feel the same satisfaction he had given me countless times.

I took him into my mouth again with vigor, quickening my speed, rubbing him, sucking him. He was warm and wet. A light pulse deep within him revealed his load had pushed closer to the edge. I looked up at him, catching his feral stare.

"You gonna cum for me, baby?" I took a moment to roll my tongue over him. He moaned and thrust harder against me, surprising me. Within a few more shoves, he came. I felt the first bit of his hot cum burst into my mouth, and I quickly released him. He pulled away, tugging on himself as he came on my neck and chest. It was new and different for us. I felt dirty, but I kind of liked it.

I grabbed my t-shirt and cleaned myself up as he caught his breath. I barely finished before he tackled me, his lips consuming mine again. His mouth overtook my neck and breasts. He tugged off my sweatpants and instantly slid his fingers inside me. I was ready for him, needed him. The curling of his digits deep inside forced my nearing climax incredibly fast. Just as I was about to lose it, he removed his hands and quickly plunged deep inside, his cock twitching as he came a second time along with me. For once, I was in the lead.

"One to Two," I teased.

He eyed me curiously and then laughed. "I'm only getting started. I'll get you more here in a bit." He groaned as he rolled off of me and lay to the side.

I giggled and sighed. His fingers lightly entwined with mine, and I smiled.

"You're incredible," he whispered.

"Quit it. You're gonna make me blush." I hid my face behind my other hand.

Mysterious rolled on top of me, his lips softly brushing mine. "I truly can't stop thinking about you. What are you doing to me?" he said between kisses.

Things were gentle the rest of the night as we kept our lips plastered to each other's, his hand clasped in mine, while we made love in a lazy, slow way. My heart rate slowed as I held onto him, and I felt content with him in my arms. Then, I suddenly wished it were Liam himself, not his character. I sighed. These feelings were perplexing and a bit frightening.

Was I falling in love?

CHAPTER EIGHT

T he next workday went as expected. All of us at the firm rushed to make the final changes to the holiday section so Liam could get it to the printers. Josh arrived on time, picking up the slack for the following week's paper. Liam must not have been entirely sour about the ordeal, for he and Josh joked around in the breakroom during lunch. Maria oddly graced the workplace halls with a smile on her face the entire day. She allowed everyone to go home early once the printers received all the proper files. I caught sight of her and Josh walking out together. It made me happy to see her giddy.

"Holiday starts now!" Liam beamed as we crossed the parking lot to our cars. Maria had granted him the rest of the week off while Josh would manage the regular publication the following day. She also allowed me to work on my copy from home for the rest of the week. Her admission about her relationship with Josh seemed to put her in a good mood. I had no idea how long her behavior change would last, but I took advantage of her leniency. However, I had the problem of having to visit my family.

"For you, maybe," I scoffed.

"You can always make an excuse to avoid going back. Say you have to work or something," Liam suggested. "It sucks that you feel obligated to go somewhere that makes you miserable."

I heaved an obnoxiously loud sigh and shrugged. "Mom will only get pissed. I'll visit her this time and avoid the rest of the holidays. I mean, I lived in that place the majority of my life. I know how to survive the suffering."

"I suppose so. Still, I don't like it."

I eyed him. "Just be glad you don't have to go."

"I could," he offered.

I paused. Was he joking?

"I mean, if you wanted me to. Any time it sucks, we can get the hell out of there. You can use me as an excuse all you want." He was serious.

"Liam, they would think you and I were a thing and bombard you with a million questions. It'd be awful. Besides, I don't want you to meet those people."

"Why not?"

"Because they are annoying. They'll just ask about us getting married and having babies, and it'll cause problems. It would be awkward. All anyone wants to do in that town is start rumors and gossip. They love to paint me in a bad light, my family included."

Liam's expression fell. He seemed a bit disappointed. I wasn't sure if it was because of what I said or if he was upset about me suffering without him there to help.

"I appreciate it, though. I know you'd jump into the fire with me if I allowed it, but there's no point in us both feeling like shit this weekend."

He rubbed the back of his neck. "Yeah. I just don't like seeing you upset."

I smiled. The poor guy was getting into protective mode. "Message me all you want! Seriously! All day if you can. Anything to tear my attention away from that place. Send me pics of your visit with your family, your food, of Hector when you care for him! Oh! Reminds me." I reached into my purse, retrieving the spare key. "Just give him a heaping bowl each day. I don't expect you to stop by numerous times. If he eats it all in one sitting, that's his fault. Also…be prepared for vomit if that happens."

"Joy," Liam chuckled, taking the key from my fingers.

"Make yourself at home while I'm gone. Just don't eat all of my ice cream."

"If I do, and I probably will, I will buy you a replacement."

"Deal."

He leaned in close, and I hugged him. "I probably won't see you before you leave, so drive carefully and message me whenever you want. Okay?" His lips grazed my ear, and I shivered.

"Okay." He kissed my cheek. I know I blushed, but I didn't care about hiding it. Unable to resist the puff of his cheek as he smiled, I kissed him back. "I'll chat with you later." I got into my car.

He waved goodbye as I pulled away. During the drive to my apartment, all I could think about was how much I would miss him, and I hated myself for feeling that way.

As Thursday rolled around, my outlook on returning to my hometown hadn't improved. My mother had messaged me a few times asking about what kinds of food I wanted and depended on me to make the desserts, and of course, she was adamant that we had plenty of alcoholic beverages to last the day. Liam and I chatted throughout the week while away from work. It mainly was fun, playful banter, and playing pool and word challenges online.

The drive to my hometown was peaceful outside the areas requiring driving through cities. With the weather and holiday traffic, those moments were slightly nerve-wracking. However, once I passed the state line and entered the straightaway leading to that small town, it was nothing but me, my chill music, and the long stretch of interstate. It was nearly a twelve-hour drive that took me over thirteen and a half to travel due to the weather and rest stops. By the time I pulled into the driveway of Carl's home, the sun had long since set. I was tired and felt gross and bloated from the gas station food I had foolishly eaten along the way.

Mom saw me pull up and rushed out to see me. She gave me a quick hug and a kiss on the cheek. I inwardly sighed, feeling a bit guilty for holding so much hostility.

"Come inside! It's freezing! We ordered pizza earlier. Come grab a beer, or we have wine," she rambled as I followed her back inside the house with my small luggage.

The house was relatively new and larger than expected. As soon as we entered, a small pack of dogs rushed toward me, barking, yipping, and jumping. High-pitched shrieks filled the air as three small children ran from one end of the room to another, circling the house between the hallways and kitchen. It was a cacophony of noise that only worsened my anxiety. Carl approached us—I recognized him from my mom's photos on social media. A married couple a few years older than me sat in the living room and drank beer as they watched television. It was safe to assume they were Carl's daughter and her husband, and the screaming menagerie was his grandkids.

"Zoey! It's good to meet you finally!" Carl said. He was slightly intoxicated and a bit loud, but he seemed kind. "That's my daughter, Milly, and her husband, Joe." They waved from the couch. "Shae, Kiley, Raymond." He pointed at each child as they circled through.

"Hi!"

"Hello!"

"Yo!"

The kids each shouted as they passed by without pause. I forced a nervous smile and waved to each member introduced. I wasn't aware they were going to be present for the weekend. And for a second, I grew even more agitated. I hated meeting new people. I reassured myself that it would all be okay. Everyone seemed polite enough.

"They're staying in the basement. Your room is upstairs." Mom guided me to my room. Carl's home was much larger than any of the houses where I grew up. Perhaps Mom finally did snag a guy with money. If that was the case, I was relieved—no more hearing about the endless financial struggle she always brought up with every conversation.

"So…what does Carl do?" I asked.

"He's retired but worked for a big company that makes commercial airplanes. He was an engineer or something like that. He has lots of money. Isn't his house nice?"

I fought back the urge to roll my eyes. "Yup. Sure is."

"This is the guest room. It used to be Milly's. We fixed it up a bit this past summer."

I nodded. It looked cozy.

"Are you going to come down?" she asked.

"Actually, I'm not hungry, and I'm exhausted. I woke up early this morning and didn't sleep well. I want to shower and go to bed. I'm sure you guys will want to get up early tomorrow as usual," I said.

"You should come have a beer."

"I don't like beer."

"We can open some wine."

"It's okay. We'll have some tomorrow with dinner." I looked at the clock. It was nearly ten.

"Okay. But you promised to have a drink with me. And I have sangria for when everyone comes over on Saturday."

"Oh, everyone's coming over here?"

"Yup! Milly and the others will leave Saturday morning, and then Grandma and the family will be over that afternoon for a late lunch."

I felt my anxiety already spiking. "Okay."

"Carl will make us all breakfast tomorrow. I'll wake you up. No sleeping all day."

"All right."

Mom leaned forward and hugged me again. "All right. Night!" One of the dogs, a yippie terrier, came into the room. "Petunia thinks it's bedtime."

"Hi, Petunia," I said. The little thing was my mom's dog. She was about six years of age but seemed twice as old instead. There was always something about mom's dogs—they seemed to age quickly or develop health problems early in life. It was typical of the general vibe that surrounded everything in the town. Petunia wheezed and waddled toward me, about fifteen pounds overweight. I scratched the dog's back, and it groaned, snorting and sneezing.

Mom exited the room, calling to her furry companion. "Come on, Petunia. You can't stay in here. Let's go watch TV."

I waved as she shut the door. Silence followed. I looked about the room, took a deep, slow breath, hopped onto the bed, and grabbed my phone. I barely looked at it during my travel, didn't like to text and drive, and only gave Liam updates at rest stops or stop signs.

'Home.' I typed.

Liam practically lived on his phone. The message was immediately read, and he responded. *'Took you long enough. How is it?'*

'Loud and intrusive. Carl's family is here too—three very young and loud children in the mix with a pack of barking dogs. Mom's already tipsy. Probably will be drunk here soon.'

'Welcome home!' Liam texted.

'Yeah. No surprise, really. BRB. I'm gonna shower.'

I didn't have to look at my phone as I knew Liam would make a suggestive response to my message. I cleaned up and got cozy in my pajamas. My room was cold, but the blankets were warm and inviting. At least I had that much.

I texted Liam for the rest of the night. We challenged each other to various games on our phones until I fell asleep.

I dreamt of him—the two of us kissing and making love in his room. It was a nice dream while it lasted. As things got good, I awoke to the stabbing sensation of puppy claws digging into my arm. Petunia hopped, darted across the bed, licked, and snorted all over me. It was mom's way of waking me up—typical procedure.

"Carl's got breakfast about made. Everyone's awake. You should come down," Mom said in a loud voice. She flicked on the bedroom light, blinding me.

I groaned and pinned Petunia down beside me. The dog was neurotic. "Okay," I grumbled with my eyes shut.

I dressed, brushed my teeth, and apprehensively met with the others downstairs. The kids were outside, playing tag. Carl had made omelets and biscuits. I quietly ate while everyone talked about their everyday lives. I participated a bit. I didn't want to be rude, but I honestly didn't care and just wanted to go home. I berated myself for my social anxiety. Then, it happened.

"So, Zoey. Do you have any kids?" Milly asked.

I cringed. "Uh…no."

Why wouldn't anyone clue her in on this?

"Oh, I knew you were married. I just wondered if you two ever had kids," she continued.

"Nope, just a cat." I smirked.

"Any plans for kids?"

"Uh…maybe. Someday."

Mom interjected. "I'll never be a grandma!"

Okay. I had enough. I stood up and cleaned off my plate. "Well, good thing Milly has a few for you to spoil. I'm going to the store to get stuff for dessert." I didn't mind cooking and prepping. If I were busy in the kitchen,

I wouldn't be forced to sit in the living room and socialize all morning, reiterating the same conversation I had for years.

"Oh, do you need money?" Mom asked.

"Nope. I got it." I rushed up the stairs and grabbed my purse. The store wasn't far, and it was pleasant outside for a change as the wind had uncharacteristically died down. I took advantage of the opportunity. A nice walk would maybe do me some good and keep me out of the house a bit longer.

However, my anxiety took over as I walked to the store and entered Main Street. I realized many people still lived in this town who I did not want to see, who were once friends but removed from my life due to toxicity or their everyday need to spread rumors about me.

I reassured myself that I would be fine. I just had to keep walking, look straight ahead, grab what I needed and leave. I thought I would be fine and believed that I could manage something so simple after improving my mental health and taking anxiety meds. It was just a trip to the grocery store, for Christ's sake. Except it wasn't any typical grocery store. I had no issues with this in the city, only here.

I walked past the old café I had once worked at in high school. Memories of past friendships, boyfriends, and work incidents flooded my mind. These were all things I had managed to block out the past two years after I left. I hurried across the street, ducking into the grocery store just as a car passed, the occupants being a couple I had grown up with who had been together since the eighth grade.

The bell to the grocery store signaled my arrival, and nearly every head in the store turned to look at me. Dear god. What had I done? I recognized just about every face in the joint. I lowered my head and grabbed a basket.

Aisle one, I seized the cream cheese. Aisle three held the pudding. I couldn't find graham crackers, so I snagged a premade crust. I needed chocolate chips, which, for some reason, wasn't with the rest of the baking supplies.

"Isn't that Zoey?" I heard a whisper. I froze, keeping my gaze locked on the cereal boxes beside me.

"I think it is. I thought she moved away."

"She did…unless she's back together with Mason."

"I thought they were still together; she just worked elsewhere. Did they ever get that divorce?"

"I heard they're still together; she's just been sleeping around with other guys in the city. He pays for everything. She's just using him."

"No, they are divorced. She was cheating on him. That's why she moved away. She ran off with her boy-toy."

"Mason hasn't even tried dating anyone else. He's still in love with her. He's so nice. I can't believe she'd do that."

Lies. They were all lies. My teeth gnashed together as it took every last bit of my patience not to retaliate. I motioned for the front, grabbing the blasted chocolate chips as I neared the end of the aisle.

Whispers surrounded me. In all this time, people still believed we were together. Mason and his family would never admit there was a problem and imagined that I would just come back home someday, and everything would fall back into place as if nothing had ever happened. I darted to the front of the line, running into a cart as it spun around the corner.

"Oh! Sorry!" I froze at the sound of the man's voice.

Kill me. Kill me now.

"Zoey?" Of all the people in this town, I had just run into my ex-husband.

"Mason!" I gasped.

"I didn't know you were coming home." Mason looked shocked, almost hurt by the sight of me. His large green eyes gazed upon me. He had gained weight. His beard was longer than ever, as was his hair, which splayed in all directions outside his ball cap.

"Yeah. Last minute," I replied. I quickly laid my items out on the checkout counter. He placed his groceries behind mine.

"Your mom?" he asked.

"Yeah."

"She drunk yet?" he knowingly quipped.

I gave a small laugh. "Probably will be by the time I get home. You…still living with your brother?"

"Naw. I got my own place closer to work. I'm a manager now."

"Oh! Well, that's good. You deserve that."

"Yeah. It's good. Finally, saving up money."

I nodded. "Yeah. Me too."

The cashier looked at each of us. "Spending the holiday together? It's so nice to see you two. How are you, Zoey? It's been forever."

"Uh, no. I'm visiting my mom. It's good. I will be leaving on Sunday. Just a short stay." I stammered more information than the woman needed to hear.

"Sunday?" Mason asked. "What are your plans for tomorrow? You can stop by for a bit at my mom's place. She wants to have dinner with everyone."

I wanted to scream. "No. Um, my family's thing is tomorrow."

I paid for my food, quickly snatching my bags. Mason eyed the front of the store. "Did you walk?"

"Yeah!" I headed for the door.

"Wait, just one second, I'll give you a ride."

I paused. Mason looked desperate for a word with me. "It's not far. I'm okay," I reassured him.

He quickly paid for his groceries and rushed to my side. He opened the door, and I flew outside with him in tow. I guess I was getting a ride home.

No, I couldn't. They would invite him over for dinner if everyone saw him pull up.

"Listen, Mason…it's…nice seeing you. But I want to walk home."

He eyed every direction. "You don't wanna be seen with me?" he asked with his slight redneck inflection. I hadn't noticed how prevalent the accent was while I lived here. Had I sounded like that at one time?

"It's just…if my mom sees you, she will harass me the rest of the day."

He nodded.

"You can message me. But I don't want to go to your mom's. I don't even want to be in this town."

"Why do you think it's so bad?"

I scoffed. "Are you kidding me? I couldn't even buy ingredients for my dessert without hearing twenty rumors about me! Rumors that you haven't managed to snuff because you can't admit to anyone that we've been divorced for over two years!" I was pissed. The past rage still boiled inside me, and I thought I had gotten over it. "I should have never come back. This place is nothing more than a pit of misery."

"So, you just hate me and everyone else," he bitterly snapped.

"Not you, but pretty much, yeah. And you know it. This place is not good for me. Nothing but bad memories."

He lowered his head in defeat. "I know."

I walked toward his old truck. It was filthy, and the tires were nearly bald. "You got to take care of your shit, Mason. You have to take care of yourself."

"I don't really have any reason to."

"Well, I'm not here to do it for you."

"I know," he mumbled. Tears stung my eyes, and I hugged him. He gripped me tightly. "I miss you," he murmured against my shoulder.

"I know you do. And I…I miss you." It wasn't a lie. I did miss him a lot. But I had to do what I did to save myself. "You know I can't stay here."

"I know."

"And I'm doing much better now."

"You look it."

"I gotta go, Mason. Get your car fixed and cleaned up. Cut your hair, please."

He laughed and quickly brightened. Mason never stayed down for long. It eased me to know that he'd be okay. I forced a smile and quickly walked away as more customers left the building, not wanting to get trapped in another conversation. As I looked back, he pulled out of his parking space, waving at me in a weird, silly way—a tradition we once had. I responded similarly, and it hurt.

"I hate this place," I whispered as I quickly sped-walked home.

I was relieved as I entered Carl's house, thinking the worst was over. However, I was wrong.

"Were you with Mason?" My mother called from the living room.

"What?" I gaped at her in awe. How on earth would she even know that?

"Roxanne just messaged me and said she saw you and Mason together. Is he coming over for dinner?"

It took every fiber of my being to maintain my composure. As I strolled into the kitchen, I said as nicely as possible, "No, Mom. Why the hell would he come here?"

"I think you should invite him. You know, he's still family. He's always welcome here."

Carl sat in a chair in the dining room, sipping scotch while smoking. "Yeah! I've met him before. He's a nice guy. I wouldn't mind him coming over. We could have a cigar together!"

I moved into the kitchen, preparing the dessert. I tossed a few bowls on the countertop, searching the drawers for a hand mixer. "No. He doesn't need to come. He has his own family plans."

"You should text him," Mom pressed. She already had a beer in her hand.

I didn't respond.

"I'll text him," she added.

"Mom!" I barked. "No! Why the hell does everyone want him around? We are done! We aren't together! I did not come here to play house and pretend everything is back to how it was."

Mom stomped into the kitchen. "Don't yell! You are being rude!"

"You all are being rude because you never think about my feelings. It's always about him and what he wants. That's all it's ever been! Why the fuck would I want to spend the holidays with my ex? Or his family? What the hell is wrong with this town?!"

"I'm getting you some wine."

"I don't want wine…." I snarled. "I just want to make this stupid dessert and get through this weekend so I can go back home to a sane environment."

I quickly mixed the pudding and cheesecake batter as my mother struggled to open a bottle of wine. It was barely noon, and she would be drinking the remainder of the day. She handed me a glass, and I took a large gulp. The first drink went down quickly. I didn't want alcohol. I just wanted things to be normal for once, not a nightmare, but I knew there was no other way I could soften the mental torment. As I finished the dessert and tossed it in the fridge to chill, my phone flashed. Liam had sent me a message.

"Who's that?" Mom asked.

"My coworker." I quickly grabbed my phone and read his message that asked how the day was going. "Oh, looks like I need to call him," I lied. "He's, uh, watching Hector this weekend."

"Is he cute?"

"What?"

"Your coworker. Is he cute?" Mom droned.

"Yeah, kinda," I muttered as I rushed through the kitchen and living room toward the stairs. I didn't care; I needed to talk to someone rational. I dialed his number and pressed the phone to my ear as I ran up the steps toward my room.

"Zoey?" Liam's voice rang through the speaker, and I suddenly felt tears sting my eyes.

"Liam!" My voice was louder than intended.

"You okay? You never call."

"I just…needed…someone else to talk to."

"It's going shitty, isn't it?" he asked.

A lump formed in my throat, and I suddenly felt incredibly vulnerable. I hated it. I loathed it. I felt weak. I did not like sharing my anxiety or depression with anyone else.

"Uh, yeah," I said with a shaky voice. "I already had a glass of wine."

"Zoey, you don't sound good. What happened?"

I repeatedly chanted in my head, 'Don't cry,' trying not to cave from the stress.

I cleared my throat. "I uh…ran into Mason uptown."

Liam remained silent for a moment. "Oh. How'd that go?"

"About as well as expected with all the people surrounding us, listening to our conversation. And now, Mom wants me to invite him over for dinner."

"What?" Liam sounded about as dumbfounded as I did about the situation. "Why the hell would you do that?"

"I know, right?!" I sighed and dropped onto the bed, pressing my fingers against my forehead. "This was a bad idea."

"Can you come home earlier?" he asked.

"God, I'm so tempted, you know."

"We can think of something. An excuse to get you out of there."

"I can't. It would piss off mom."

"Screw your mom, Zoey! All of them!" Liam cursed. "I knew this wouldn't be good for you, going back there. I should have kept you from leaving."

I gave a short laugh. Liam was a bit overprotective at times. "It'll be okay. I mean, I grew up here with all these people."

"Doesn't mean you should suffer any longer. That place is toxic. It never does you any good."

I rubbed my forehead. "I know. I really fucking wish I stayed home."

"Well…just talk to me for a while until you have your dinner."

I relaxed into the bed, feeling sleepy. The anxiety and glass of wine did nothing but tire my system. "Okay," I said with a yawn.

"You're crashing now, aren't you?" he chuckled.

"Naw."

We spoke for a bit. Liam talked about his visit with Hector and how they bonded and had "bro time." He joked about trying on my clothes and eating all my snacks. I giggled, and the sound of his voice eased my nerves. I hadn't realized how tense I was. Before I knew it, there was a knock at the door, and I jolted awake. I had fallen asleep while Liam chattered on the phone. I noticed the call had ended not long ago, but the time was a couple of hours after I nodded off.

"Zoey?" Mom opened the door.

I looked over my shoulder, my hair falling in front of my eyes.

"Did you fall asleep?" she asked with a drunken giggle.

"I did," I said, sitting up. I wiped the edge of my mouth. I must have passed out hard, for I had drooled.

"Carl's got the food heating in the oven. Come have some drinks with us."

I quickly grabbed my phone and unenthusiastically followed her downstairs, where Carl, Milly, and Joe conversed with small glasses of whiskey in their hands in the dining room as the children shouted and played games in the living room.

I quickly texted Liam. *'You stayed on the phone while I slept.'*

'You talk in your sleep,' he replied. *'You're adorable.'*

'Creeper.'

Thankfully, the rest of the evening went relatively fast, probably partly due to the entire bottle of wine I consumed. I dodged many personal questions at dinner. Milly mostly talked with Carl, and Mom sometimes joined in. Joe was awkward and quiet. He turned in his chair to watch the television throughout. The kids ate at a smaller table in the living room, giggling and chatting about school and toys.

"Play with us!" The youngest one, Raymond, shouted, tugging on my arm.

Truthfully, I liked kids. And all who were present were of the ages I enjoyed the most. Kids were funny, witty, and far more aware than adults. I used it as an excuse to leave the table, as I often did in the presence of obnoxious adults and their children during holidays and barbeques. However, it had been far too long since I held a child or played with one.

"What are you guys playing?" I asked.

They had a gaming system connected to the television. Each kid held a separate controller.

"Bowling!" they screamed.

"Okay, okay. I know how to do this one," I said, taking a position in the center of the room.

We took turns playing. Laughing and being silly was lovely, and I suddenly felt better. Liam would have loved it. My smile faltered. For a moment, I had wished he were with the kids and me. He was great with children.

I grabbed my phone as the kids fussed over what to play next. Opening a photo app on my phone, I grabbed the small boy and posed with him, using various filters that gave us bunny ears and giant mouths. I was bombarded by the other two, and we spent a good half hour taking videos and pics. I sent them all to Liam.

'Drunk Zoey with kids. Interesting,' he responded.

Soon, he started sending photos back. The kids loved it.

"Is that your boyfriend?" the eldest girl, Shae, exclaimed.

"Um…no…well…." I paused. What on earth were we?

"He's cute!" Kiley agreed, and they giggled.

"He's not cute; he's handsome!" Raymond sneered. "Men aren't cute."

"Who are you talking about?" My mom interrupted. Suddenly, all the fun in the room was sucked out like a vacuum in space.

"Zoey's boyfriend!" Shae and Kiley simultaneously chimed.

"You have a boyfriend?" she asked.

"Come on, kids, time for bed!" Milly shouted. "We have to leave early in the morning."

The room erupted with a myriad of complaints. I took the opportunity to ignore my mother's question, shutting down the TV and gaming system.

"Goodnight, Zoey!" The kids each took turns hugging me.

As they left, the room fell into an awkward silence. I moved toward the stairs, messaging Liam. "Man, that wine and those kids have knocked me out! I am exhausted." I faked a yawn.

"Who is your boyfriend?" she sternly asked.

"Liam. My coworker." I faced her, matching her tone.

"Why didn't you tell me about him?"

"He's the same Liam I've worked with for the past two years. You already know about him."

"Is he the cute one?"

I ground my teeth together. "Yeah." I knew what she meant and didn't want to hear her next question.

"Well, does he make good money? Can he support you?"

"Mom, we're just dating, not getting married. Besides, I'm not getting married again. That was a disaster I'd rather avoid in the future. I mean, we're not even dating! We're just friends."

"Why didn't you bring him here for everyone to meet?" she asked.

"Because I don't want to bring him here. That would be torture."

"Why are you so mean?" she snipped.

"Why do you suddenly care? I haven't heard from you in six months, and now you want to know all about my life and have me visit?" The wine had made me a bit bold. I didn't care about anything at the moment.

"You never talk to me!" she argued.

"You never talk to me! You don't message. You don't care about anything that I do. Do you even know where I work or what I do? Do you even know where I live?"

She folded her arms, sulking.

"I don't want to bring Liam here and make him go through the torment of twenty questions with every nosey person in this town and our family. Especially when he and I aren't even a thing." I started up the stairs.

"You can bring him for Christmas," Mom sputtered.

"No," was my short response. "I'm going to bed."

"I'll wake you up for breakfast," she said as if she suddenly forgot the conversation. "Let's go to bed, Petunia!"

I heaved an irritable sigh and quickly shut the door to my room, demanding privacy.

'Mom's drunk. I'm…feeling shitty. Kids are in bed.'

'Aw, fun time's over?' Liam messaged.

'Those kids literally saved me tonight. I forgot I was in hell for a short amount of time.'

'Well, one day down, right?'

'I dunno how I can last another day.' I quickly pulled off my shirt, wanting to shower before settling into bed. I only desired to talk with Liam the rest of

the night until I fell asleep. I hated that I needed him to help keep my mind straight. In a rush, I washed off my makeup, brushed my teeth, and showered in record time. As I settled into bed, I swallowed a pill to help prevent a hangover. I sipped on my water and checked my notifications on social media.

'What are you doing now?' he asked.

'Thinking about me?' I responded.

'All day.'

I stared at the message, grinning like an idiot. *'Miss me?'*

'Of course.'

A mischievous attitude took over me, and I suddenly felt very playful. *'Which part?'*

I could see he was typing a reply. The dotted bubble bobbed a few times, disappeared, bounced again, and vanished. He had trouble producing a response.

'Is this a trick question?' he finally asked.

'No.'

'All of you.'

I snickered. *'In what way?'*

'Your kiss. I keep thinking about that.'

'You miss these lips?'

'Your lips, your smile, the curve of your ass.'

'Oh, Liam talking dirty.' With an awkward twist, I snapped a shot of my behind. I wore a T-shirt and a pair of panties, nothing else. Without hesitation, I sent the image to him.

A series of multiple emoticons and hilarious gifs flooded my messenger.

'Was not expecting that, but I am NOT complaining,' he wrote. *'Send more.'*

'What would you like to see?'

The messenger fell silent a moment. I felt my heart racing. It was exhilarating flirting with Liam like this.

'I have no idea. I'm just trying not to die right now,' he wrote.

I snapped a selfie and sent it to him. Then, I took a few more provocative shots, one of my cleavage, and picked and edited the photos I liked, sending them to him one after another.

'How's that?' I asked.

It took a moment, but he responded with a picture. I gasped. He had sent a shot of his lower half covered in briefs but with a firm erection beneath. I licked my lips and took a sip of water, feeling excited by the sight.

'We should play.' I typed.

'How drunk are you? I don't want to take advantage of this situation.'

I frowned. *'Aw, so sweet. Shut up, Liam. I'm fine. Let's play.'*

'Yes, Ma'am!'

'What would you do if I were there?'

Liam's messages halted a bit, but then the text bubble bounced for a while. It had been a long time since I had sex chatted with someone. I wondered how good he would be at it.

'I would start by kissing you. Touching the side of your face, brushing my fingers through your soft hair,' he replied.

A crooked grin spread across my face as I got comfortable beneath the covers. I regretted not having my vibrator with me. I didn't even think about the possibility of needing it.

'I would love to taste your lips. Feel your body with my hands. Slip my hand into your waistband, teasing you, tickling you,' I responded.

'Mmm, that sounds nice.'

'How's that erection?'

I received a picture. There was Liam's rock-hard cock in all its glory, the tip leaking with precum. I clenched my thighs. God, how badly I wanted him.

I messaged that I desperately craved to touch him, feel him twitch in my hand. He was slick, and I wanted to play with his tip and make him squirm. Taste him. Squeeze him. I sent him a photo of my hand slipping into my panties.

A video popped up. It was Liam touching and gently stroking himself.

'You've got me SO hard,' he wrote.

'Send me more of you playing. I want to see you cum.' I demanded.

I watched his video repeatedly as I waited and realized something—Mysterious and I were always in the pitch dark. I never got to see him in great detail. But this time, Liam revealed all his intimate parts to me, illuminated by the soft orange light of his bedside lamp.

Another video popped up, and I saw the curve of his abdomen. Long fingers trailed over his stomach and settled along his tip. He teased himself for me. I turned up the volume and heard his increased breathing, and I touched myself as I watched.

"Do you want this?" he asked in the video as he caressed himself.

"Oh, god, yes," I responded aloud despite his inability to hear.

"Hm?" His thumb trailed over his head, and as he pulled away, a strand of thick precum followed with it.

I watched as Liam tugged himself, moaning as he quickened his pace. Just as things were about to get good, the phone lit up with a call. He wanted to video chat.

A blush burned my cheeks, and I looked back and forth. I quickly hopped up, turned off the bedroom light, and pounced back into bed, turning on the bedside lamp. I pressed on the phone screen, answering Liam's call.

"Hey," I said in a muffled voice.

"I can't stand these long wait times between messages and videos." I saw his face, and I paused, staring in awe. His hair was messy, undoubtedly fussed with due to his sexual frustration. With dilated pupils and a heaving bare chest, he looked wild and unbelievably sexy. "Let me finish with you. I want to see you, too."

I grinned and bit my lip.

"God, you are sexy," he said in a raspy voice.

Hearing him say it in his natural voice and not with an accent gave me chills.

"So are you. I wish I were there," I said, keeping my voice down.

"I would ravage you," he purred.

Without much else to say, he flipped his camera around, giving me a video of his full erection. I did the same, showing him my lower belly.

"I wish I had my toy." A tiny giggle betrayed my confidence.

"Fuck. That would be so hot."

Hearing him talk in such a way as Liam was new and exciting.

"Guess you'll have to make do with your fingers," he said.

He touched himself, and I did the same. I hummed, and he followed with a similar sound. Up, down, up, down, his hand traveled over his flesh. I was amazed at his look, drawn in by the raw, sexual image.

"I honestly won't last long. This is all surprising as hell," he whispered.

"Yeah, same," I said with a sharp breath.

"Will you cum for me?" he asked politely.

I laughed. "Yeah! But you gotta cum too."

I watched as he moved faster and faster, his breaths quickening. I slid my fingers inside myself with a gasp, playing with the folds, giving him a closer view. I heard a grunt, and his hand pulsed quickly over his tip.

"Yes," I hissed. "Give it to me."

Gasp, gasp, a quick moan, and he came. My release immediately followed. It was insanely hot watching his climax. One, two, three, four bursts of hot white fluid shot up toward the camera. Keeping my mouth shut, I quieted my sounds of pleasure so I wouldn't wake the entire house. My moans softly merged with the sound of his. I slowed my massage as his camera panned over his body, showing the trail of cum that decorated his abdomen and chest.

"Shit!" he murmured and laughed. "It got on my pillow."

Sure enough, a wet spot was beside his neck, soaking the cloth of his pillowcase. I wished I had it all recorded on video to replay later, but the live feed was just as good for now. We shyly laughed and took the time to clean up. Afterward, we both aimed our cameras at our faces. I curled up and hugged my pillow.

"Hm," he took a deep breath and gazed at me with sleepy eyes. "That…was awesome."

"It was."

He yawned, causing me to do the same. I suddenly realized how tired I was despite my earlier nap.

"I'm beat," he said.

"Same."

"Too bad you're over there. I would cuddle the shit out of you if you were here."

I smirked at the idea. "That sounds good right now."

"When you get home…we'll do that."

"Cuddle?"

"Yeah. You can come over, and I will cuddle you all night." He wiggled his fingers. "I'll pet you to sleep."

"Promise?" I asked through my smile.

His grin matched mine. "Promise."

I made a quiet purr and closed my eyes. I didn't want to hang up, so I pretended Liam was in bed with me. With a peek, I saw that he lay with his eyes closed and his lips twisted into a relaxed smile. The sight was comforting, and I closed mine again, pretending I was curled up against his chest.

"Goodnight, Zoey," I heard him whisper.

"Night night…" I barely managed to say before I fell fast asleep.

I purposefully woke up late the following day to avoid interactions I didn't want. However, my mother dragged me from my bedroom to prepare for the mid-afternoon lunch involving the rest of my family members. I helped out in the kitchen as my relatives slowly entered the house, the noise growing louder each second as everyone tried to speak over one another about the latest news they had heard.

"Zoey's here? Where's Zoey?" I waited in the kitchen for my grandmother to pass the threshold. I smiled and quickly lifted a hand towel before my face, hiding as she shuffled in. "Ah! Is that my Zoey?!"

I laughed and lowered the cloth. "Hi, Grandma!"

My grandma was one of the few people who supported my moving to the city. She was a short, round woman who loved to wear pastels and floral patterns. When she hugged someone, there was nowhere to go but into her breasts. As her arms pulled me into a tight embrace, I awaited impact, her strength momentous for her size. Groaning, I giggled at the sound of her infectious laughter.

"I missed you," she said.

"Missed you too," I replied.

She gazed over the freshly baked cinnamon rolls I had made from scratch. Grandma taught me all I knew about cooking. I spent most of my summers with her and Grandpa on their farm. Painting, cooking, sewing, she taught me everything.

"These are for me?" she questioned, pointing at the plump rolls.

"All of them." I nodded.

She giggled and picked one up, biting into it. With a 'shhh,' she winked and wobbled around the house, greeting the family members as they entered.

"Zoey!" I cringed at the new, intrusive voice. Grandma was probably the only person I missed, but in strolled Candy, my mother's cousin. She was tall, lanky, nosey, gossipy, and was one I couldn't stand to be around.

"Hi, Candy," I politely stated as we gave each other a small sideways hug.

She looked around with her lips tightly pursed. "Where's Mason?" she asked.

Right…to…the point. I looked away and continued prepping, trying to decide what to say.

"Why would Mason be here?" Grandma called out from the dining room.

"Well, I just figured he would be here since Zoey was in town too."

"No, Mason will not be here. He's got his own family to do things with," I said.

The doorbell rang, and there came a sudden commotion. "Mason!" Many voices shouted.

I froze. What in the hell was going on?

"Hello!" I heard Mason's voice.

Immediately, my chest tightened. My muscles tensed, goosebumps covering my arms. I felt the blood drain from my face, struggling with my breath. With a cautious step, I entered the living room with my hands clasped before my breast. There, my entire family sang their hellos and embraced my ex-husband. He gazed at me, and his smile fell. He knew.

"Why is he here?" I barely managed to ask.

"I figured I'd invite him over since you were in town. I thought it would be nice for you two," my mother said.

I glared at her, no longer capable of hiding my displeasure. Each year, it was increasingly difficult to hide behind the fake smiles that once dominated my life. I had to pass by everyone to get to the staircase—my cousins, aunts, uncles, grandmother, and Carl.

"She said you wanted me here." Mason followed me.

I didn't care that he tagged along. I wasn't mad at him. "No, Mason." Taking a deep breath as I climbed the steps toward my room, I recalculated my response. "It's not like I don't want you here. I don't hate you."

He watched as I tossed all my things into my suitcase. My hands shook, and I grabbed my medication, taking one of the white pills for my anxiety.

"If it were just you and I, it would be different. But it's not. It's with them. They have always loved you and only cared about you anyway. And that's fine! I don't want them to hate you, but they all act like they hate me and enjoy…literally *enjoy* harassing me."

"I knew I should have texted you about it before I came over," he somberly stated. He knew all about my mother and her ways, about how much my family stressed me out. "Are you leaving?"

"Yeah!" I exclaimed, tears stinging my eyes. "I can't deal with this. I thought I could, but I just can't!"

I felt like hyperventilating, and I berated myself for getting so bad. I hadn't had a panic attack like this in a long time. As I gazed at Mason, he looked at me with saddened eyes. He had dressed up for dinner, wearing a button-up flannel shirt and new jeans, and had even cut his dirty-blonde hair and trimmed his beard.

"Then you get out of here. I'll walk with you," he said with his slight drawl.

I nodded and grabbed my suitcase, purse, and phone. Together, we walked down the stairs. It was like 'the walk of shame.' We beelined for the door, and my mother hopped up, exclaiming, "Where are you going?!"

"I gotta go," I quickly said as Mason opened the front door for me. I could hear the whispers and mumbles behind me.

"You can't leave! Everyone wants to see you," she stammered.

"No, mom! They don't give a fuck about seeing me. They want to see Mason!"

Mason kept calm and loaded my luggage as I spoke to her.

"That's not true. You are being rude!" she yelled.

"Zoey," Grandma called from the front porch.

I frowned. If I didn't leave soon, I was going to start crying.

With a smile, my grandmother waved and said, "You drive safe. Call me sometime, okay?"

I felt a bit of relief and nodded. "Okay. Love you, grandma."

"What am I going to tell everyone? I invited Mason because you were here. You're being rude to him," Mom continued.

Mason slammed the back door of my vehicle. "No offense, but I don't give a shit about dinner. I only came because I thought Zoey wanted me here. And I know she doesn't hate me, but you are good at putting her in situations to make her look bad. I don't know why. I don't know if it's because you feel like it gives you attention, but nobody likes it."

"Leave them alone, Nancy," Grandma called out.

"Well! This is just embarrassing!" My mom started throwing a tantrum, stomping her feet like a child.

I sighed and quickly moved to the driver's side. Mason met me there, and I hugged him.

"You can call me any time," he said.

"I know," I spoke against his shoulder.

"Get out of here before she makes things worse," he whispered.

I complied and entered my vehicle. Mason waved at me, nodded at my grandmother, and ignored my mother's antics as he climbed into his truck and departed. I waited for him to pull away before quickly backing out of the driveway. As I gasped for air, I pulled into the gas station on the edge of town, screaming in frustration. I grabbed my cell phone and immediately messaged Liam.

'Leaving. Mom invited Mason. Everything got fucked up. Mason was cool with it and helped me leave. I'm driving home tonight. Won't be home until really late.'

I entered the gas station with shaking hands and purchased a coffee and a soggy sandwich to hold me over. I wouldn't feel any better until I drove out of town. Before I pulled away, I read Liam's response.

'What?! Why did she do that? Okay. Message me when you can so I know you are safe.'

'Because she's insane,' was all I wrote.

'Come over tomorrow. I'll make you dinner. Seriously, we'll have our own Thanksgiving. You deserve a delicious meal and relaxation.'

I almost cried at his request. It sounded so lovely. *'Okay. I'll message you later.'*

I didn't bother to look back as I exited the town and entered the highway. Who knew when I would return, but at that moment, I never wanted to.

CHAPTER NINE

LIAM

The day started dull. I both loved and hated having vacation time. For one, I didn't have to work, which was awesome! However, since there was no work, I had nothing to do. I wasn't particularly good at entertaining myself at home. There was only so much television and gaming I could endure before I felt sick from not being productive. Thankfully, I had chores to do thanks to Zoey—an excuse to leave my apartment.

The ride was relatively short. We didn't live too far apart, and the weather cooperated enough that the roads were finally clear of the slick sludge of ice and snow. I had nothing planned outside of my family's dinner, which had been on Thanksgiving Day, while Zoey took to the road. It was as expected. Dinner with my parents, sister, brother, and their spouses and children consisted of delicious food and conversation, and overall, it was quite pleasant. It made me feel guilty because I knew the exact opposite was happening for Zoey.

I gazed at my phone on Saturday afternoon. I hadn't heard from her much since our video chat session. The thought made my throat dry. Those sultry events had been far more than I expected. But with her teasing pictures, I couldn't help myself. She was so damn sexy, and she would never realize how much her stunning eyes, blonde hair, and curves turned me on. No matter how often I told her she was beautiful, I knew there was always doubt in her mind. It drove me up the wall.

Entering her apartment, Hector greeted me. The cat trotted to the door, green eyes large and hopeful. As soon as he saw me, the light dimmed in his irises, and he gave a soft meow, prancing toward his food bowl.

"Yeah, I know, buddy. It's only me. Mama won't be home until tomorrow," I told the cat.

After tossing a scoop of food into Hector's bowl and refilling his water, I moseyed to Zoey's couch. I felt terrible about only feeding the cat and then running off, so I made it a point to hang out to prevent the animal's loneliness. Though, I'm not sure how much he cared about it. I yawned as I turned on the television, checking out what streaming services she had. I had no plans for the night, and my other friends were out of town, so I decided to catch a show or two with Hector. It was about the best I could do. Besides, drinking alone at Ronnie's bar was miserable, especially this time of year.

Hector hopped onto the cushions, eyeballing me.

"What's up, dude?"

"Meow," was all he said before he sprang onto the back of the sofa a second time and curled into a ball.

"Okay. You hang out there, and I'll pick a show." I scrolled through the options. "Zombies?" Hector opened one eye but didn't say anything. "Cowboys?" Nothing. "Aliens?" Quiet still. "We're running out of options, buddy. Oh! How about this one? It has a bit of everything, including…*dragons*."

"Meow."

"Ah, there we go. Let's watch this one."

We got a few episodes in before I awoke to a loud chime on my phone. I fell asleep during one of the best parts. I hadn't seen the show but knew enough of the plot, thanks to spoilers on social media. Hector had moved to lay on my legs, and I felt joy ripple through my heart. That was a huge accomplishment. Zoey said Hector didn't like men.

I reached for my phone, which had fallen on the floor. Judging by the notification's color lighting up, I knew it was her. The app we chatted on differed from what I used for most people, but Zoey enjoyed it as she could send me pictures using ridiculous filters. Swiping open my phone's home screen, I tapped on her name, ignoring the others. I always checked her notifications first, even before my mother's. I read her message and frowned.

'Leaving. Mom invited Mason. Everything got fucked up. Mason was cool with it and helped me leave. I'm driving home tonight. Won't be home until really late.'

"Holy shit. What the fuck?" I murmured. Hector chirped at me, and I swiftly responded.

'What?! Why did she do that? Okay. Message me when you can so I know you are safe.'

I waited for what felt like an eternity, staring at the messages, waiting for her icon to appear and reveal that she was typing a response. The suspense was killing me.

'Because she's insane,' was all she wrote.

I sighed. Zoey did have the worst kind of luck with these types of things. I didn't believe her at first, but after knowing her for this long, it was apparent that terrible things happened to her, often because of weird and controlling people. I was more angry than sad about it. Zoey was a brilliant, creative, and beautiful young woman. She deserved a life that made her smile every day. Then, I had an idea and hastily replied.

'Come over tomorrow. I'll make you dinner. Seriously, we'll have our own Thanksgiving. You deserve a good meal and relaxation.'

I waited for her response, wondering if she would want something like that or prefer to be left alone.

'Okay. I'll message you later.' She didn't write more after that, and I knew she would be driving throughout the night.

A massive sense of relief washed over me. I now had something to do for Sunday, and I would get to see her again. A smile crossed my face. I'd make her a nice dinner and provide a relaxing atmosphere. Then, I thought about other sexual possibilities. Would she want to try Codeword: Mystery if we were at my place? Or would she prefer it to be me as myself? I made a mental note to prepare for our game.

"I have a date with your mama tomorrow at my place. Would that be okay, dude?" I looked toward Hector.

"Meaaah," it was a strange purring mew, but I took it as a 'yes.'

"Right on," I said, grinning.

We watched a few more episodes of the show, eating the rest of Zoey's ice cream before I grew bored. The sun had set, and I didn't want to risk falling asleep again. I had to get home and get ready for her surprise. I gave Hector an extra dose of food and patted him a few times before leaving.

My mind was a whirlwind of possibilities. What was her favorite food? I didn't have a turkey or any traditional Thanksgiving dinner food. However, I had a bottle of wine, and though I didn't have any sweets, I did have the ingredients to make brownies. I also needed to clean. Suddenly, I felt nervous. She'd been over plenty of times, but this was special and different.

As I exited her apartment, I locked the door, slipped on my coat, and turned and bumped into someone strolling past. They struck me hard, and I spun, looking at the back of the man as he hurriedly rushed toward the rear exit of the building, adjusting his hood while he slipped on his leather gloves. From the window at the end of the hallway, I noticed it had started snowing.

"Shit, sorry, man! I didn't see you," I called out.

He didn't respond but kept moving forward, pausing at the door leading to the side stairwell exit.

"Uh, yeah…happy holidays," I muttered and continued onward.

Why were people such jerks? It made me uneasy. I often tried to talk Zoey into moving into my complex. It was in a better neighborhood, and I would feel better knowing she was nearby if anything happened. Plus, there was the convenience of watching Hector any time she wanted me to without the drive, and my neighbors tended to be much friendlier.

I shook my head as I hurried toward the opposite exit. One asshole wasn't going to ruin my mood. I quickly shrugged away the negativity and entered the parking lot, only concerned with one thing—pleasing Zoey.

CHAPTER TEN

ZOEY

I pulled up to my apartment just after 4 am. Exhausted and hungry, I simply wanted to have a snack and go to bed. The snow slowed me down a bit. Luckily, it had only been a light flurry. Entering my apartment, I greeted my furball with a high-pitched voice. He called back in a similar tone, his tail straight in the air as he trotted toward me on his tiny tiptoes. Oh, how I missed Hector. I picked him up and kissed him.

"I love you, boo. Aw, it was terrible. I can't go back there. Next time, tell me to stay home, okay?" I kissed his soft, triangular head a few more times before setting him down. He meowed and ran to his bowl. "You still hungry?"

I turned on the kitchen light and eyed his bowl. There was still a light sprinkle of brown nibbles scattered around the inside.

"You still have food."

He eyed the dish and then me. The look was expectant. "Meow."

I let out an exasperated sigh, not wanting to argue. "Fine. As long as you promise to be good. I'm going straight to bed."

I dropped a small handful of food into his bowl and opened my fridge. There was a small box of pizza inside with a note from Liam.

'Leftovers. If I forget about it, dig in.'

I eagerly accepted the food and shoved a slice in my mouth. Together, we ate in the kitchen in profound silence. The energy felt weird. I shivered and looked out the window above the sink. Large flakes of snow drifted slowly outside. It felt unusually cold.

Swallowing the last bite of pizza, I grabbed a second slice before walking to the thermostat. I twisted the dial, listening to the heater startup. The dusty smell of the heat invaded my nostrils. I kicked off my shoes and reached for my nightstand lamp as I entered my bedroom.

Strong arms wrapped around my middle, and I shrieked with the food still in my mouth. Mysterious tossed me onto the bed, his dark body covering mine. Somewhere, the pizza was lost. I quickly swallowed and yelped as his warm mouth locked onto my throat, biting, kissing, sucking.

"God! You're eager tonight."

He didn't reply, but his hands swiftly worked to remove my jeans. I helped a bit, squirming upwards across the bed. Gloved fingers traveled over my thighs, up to my stomach, nearly ripping my shirt off my body. I clumsily moved with the rough handling. I was flipped over with my arm latched high and tight behind my back. I cried out as it hurt a bit.

"Easy, there."

"Quiet," he finally spoke.

I silenced myself as he removed my undergarments and abruptly entered inside me. Things had been rough before, but this felt more violent than usual, more than I ever expected him to be.

"Didn't think you'd ever show up for tonight's game," he huskily whispered.

"I said I would—"

"Quiet!"

He thrust hard inside me, keeping one hand locked on my wrists to keep my arms locked behind my back. His other hand pulled my hips up so that my back painfully arched in an extreme pose with my face smashed into the blankets. It didn't feel good; I could barely breathe and honestly didn't like it. Groaning, I bit back my disapproval.

"First, you leave town. Then you talk to another man and let him enter your apartment."

"Ah! Careful."

"Quiet," he hissed. I felt him fiddle with my wrists, and then I realized he had tied them together. His hands explored my body, roughly squeezing and pinching. "I get jealous. Very jealous."

I whimpered as he spun me around and gripped my throat. I wasn't sure what I felt. Did I enjoy it? A tingle settled in my belly as he slowed down, but he kept his hand around my neck. He was taking the roleplaying seriously tonight.

"Who do you belong to?" he asked.

I struggled to catch my breath as he pounded against me.

"Answer me," he growled, his hand tightening a bit.

"Y-you," I replied.

I could barely see him in the darkness, but the heater vent kicked up the curtains enough to spontaneously allow some streetlight from outside. A harsh glow reflected against his ghostly face paint. The shadow of his hood kept his eyes looking like empty sockets. He parted his lips, and I saw a shimmer of teeth as he moaned with desire. Perhaps we were taking our game a bit far. We never laid out any ground rules about pleasure versus pain and never designated a safe word. Truthfully, the idea never crossed my mind. I'd never imagined Liam to be a rough lover. I pushed aside the thoughts, wondering if this was also new to him.

His hips slammed into me over and over again—fast, hard. I felt him wholly, and I could already feel bruised inside. I gasped with pleasure mixed with discomfort. And after a while, it merely hurt.

"Please," I gasped. "It's hurting."

He stopped abruptly and painfully gripped my chin. "Not until I'm finished."

I was tired, my nerves were shot, and tears stung my eyes. I gasped and made loud noises, pretending to enjoy his rough dominance. Mysterious seemed to like it, smirking as he continued to have his way with me.

"Mmmm, yeah," I moaned.

I had to power through it. I had been through this situation before and faked it many times in the past.

His breaths grew quick, and his speed increased as I gave him verbal feedback. It was working. Soon, he would crumble over the edge. His hands flew to my breasts as his mouth latched onto mine. A mixture of feelings overcame me—pleasure, pain, and a bit of sadness.

Mysterious came hard. And once he was done using my body, he abruptly slipped out. I rolled to the side, refusing to look at him as he caught his breath. After a moment, I felt the sweet release of the ties around my wrists. I quickly pulled my hands to my chest, rubbing them. The heater shut off for its cycle, and the curtains stopped moving, returning the room to pitch black. The bed shifted beside me.

"I'll see you tomorrow," he whispered in my ear. Then, he pressed a gentle kiss against my temple.

I didn't say anything but remained frozen on the bed, listening to the apartment door as it quietly opened and closed. It was the first time Mystery left before I fell asleep.

I felt used and abused by everyone. I was confused and hurt. Perhaps I was overly sensitive due to the events at my mother's. Maybe I was reading into it too much. Surely, Liam didn't mean to hurt my feelings. Playing the powerful, mysterious stranger must have been part of the game. I planned to discuss it with him the following evening to lay out some rules. And then I realized that maybe I didn't want to play our game anymore. Mysterious was once a thing I craved and desired—dark, dangerous, and sexy. Right now, I only wanted Liam's soft embrace and warm words. Mysterious was the opposite, and I wasn't sure I liked that persona anymore. My mind whirled, and I thought about the possibility that perhaps that was the man Liam actually was. Maybe he was a cold, harsh lover.

Curling into the fetal position, I sobbed. I heard a quiet purr, and Hector curled beside me, his weight thumping against me as he nuzzled my hands, covering my face.

"Oh, boo bear. What do I do?" I squealed and cried against his soft black fur until I fell asleep.

I woke up incredibly late, well past noon. I rotated in bed with a grumpy groan to look at my phone. It wasn't in my room. I sighed and realized I never had the time to get ready for bed before being attacked by Mysterious.

I stumbled out of the room with little energy, readied a coffee pot, and searched my purse for my phone. Twenty messages flashed across my notification menu from various apps. A few were from my mother, which I ignored. I lifted the bar on my screen to read what Liam had written.

'Hey. Hope you got in safely last night. Hit me up when you are awake.'

'You doing okay? Just worried about you coming in so late. I imagine you're dead asleep. You can come over any time you're ready.'

Remembering last night, I exhaled long and slow.

"I'll go to his place for dinner, and when the time isn't awkward, I'll bring up the game," I softly spoke aloud.

I messaged him.

'Just woke up. Got in really late. Going to shower and get ready.'

Liam messaged as I prepared, and he seemed chipper and excited to see me. It eased my mood. He was only playing it rough last night. Liam had a gentle soul and would never purposefully hurt me. In fact, I had once mentioned I liked being tied up and was keen on possibly trying more exciting ways of having sex. We had talked about it at the bar, but I had never thought he would have that domineering air about him. The more we messaged, the better I felt about everything. I sipped my coffee as I chose my outfit.

'Do I need to dress up?' I asked.

'Naw. Wear whatever you want. I want you to be comfortable. You look good either way.'

Good, because I had no desire to dress up, especially in this miserable weather. Gusting freezing air caused the complex to moan, and I shivered at the thought. Digging through my closet and drawers, I found a thick pair of fleece-lined yoga pants and a t-shirt with a gimmicky nerd reference—comfortable. I put on makeup to cover the puffiness of my eyes from the crying I had done, and I curled my hair. Nothing too fancy, but enough to still feel cute.

"Pretty face, showing the booty." I looked in the mirror. "Good enough."

I slipped on my thick socks and dressed in leather boots and a matching jacket. I wrapped a scarf around my neck and slid on my gloves. The idea of going out in such weather was dreadful, but I needed a distraction.

I said goodbye to Hector, ensuring he was well-supplied for the day, and made my way to Liam's. I drank my coffee during the drive, realizing I had again forgotten to shut off the coffee maker. I scowled—such a waste of a tasty brew.

"Lil Zoey!" Liam exclaimed as he opened the door to his apartment. He wore jeans and a dark t-shirt with the logo of a local restaurant that served gourmet burgers and their house-made fancy beers.

A sensation of smells surrounded me as he pulled me into a hug—cleaner chemicals, air freshener, and the scents of something sweet and saucy coming from the oven. I embraced him and relaxed, recognizing his cologne.

"How are you feeling?" he asked as he pulled away.

I gave a slight shrug. "A bit tired."

"Aw, do you need any coffee?"

"Drank mine on the way here." He hung my jacket and purse on the wall beside the entryway.

Liam's apartment was nicer than mine. Graphic posters decorated the white walls; fine suede furniture and large handmade pottery vases created a rich atmosphere. Knowing Liam, he got a good deal on everything. He was frugal but maintained good taste.

"Perhaps a glass of wine? It's still a bit early, but when has that stopped us?" He entered the kitchen, where a bar separated it from the dining area.

"You know what? I think that would help," I breathed a small laugh. I was disappointed in myself for not being more cheerful.

Liam lifted a finger and nodded as he rummaged through his fridge and retrieved a bottle of my favorite cheap wine. "Red wine, which should pair well with our dinner."

I inhaled the fragrance of his cooking. "What is for dinner? It smells good."

As he pulled the cork, he smirked. "Lasagna. Breadsticks. Salad. Brownies for dessert."

"Liam! You didn't have to do so much."

He poured me a glass and clicked on a tablet on his countertop. Calm jazz music played throughout the apartment. "It wasn't any trouble. I enjoy cooking. Besides, you've given me something to do today. It was dreadfully boring while you were gone," he added dramatically.

We clinked our glasses together and took a drink. I closed my eyes, calming my nerves further, the memories of the night before pressed far back in my mind.

"Dinner is almost ready. Until then…." He set down his glass, reached for my free hand, and guided me toward him, swaying in a dance.

I giggled, appreciating all he had done to make me feel better. As we rocked, I took small sips of my wine. He leaned down, and I tilted my glass so he could share a taste. The red liquid dribbled down his chin, and as he wiped his face, I grabbed his hand and kissed away the mess. He rested his forehead against mine.

"I'm sorry things were shitty back home," he whispered.

"It's not my home. It hasn't been for years."

I pressed my cheek against his shoulder, feeling safe in his arms.

"This can be your home. You know you're always welcome here," he said. The rumble in his chest was soothing, but his words were surprising. What did he mean, exactly?

I looked up to him, locked in his grey eyes. Facial hair lined his sharp jaw. He had combed back his brown hair, and I wanted to run my fingers through it. His expression was severe yet soft. My heart pounded as he lifted a hand and gently stroked my cheek.

"I never want you to put yourself in a position where you feel harmed in any way," he whispered.

He leaned down and kissed me. Already, the wine created a buzz, and I moaned against his lips. One of his hands lightly trailed up and down my back, the other still caressing my face. He pressed against me, deepening the kiss, and I leaned back against the bar top. Despite everything, my body eagerly responded to his gentle caresses. With my fingers clenching his shirt, I pulled him even closer, our tongues swirling. His hips pushed against mine, and I felt his erection through his jeans.

The oven beeped—loud and annoying.

BEEP.

We continued.

BEEP.

His hands lowered beneath my shirt, his thumbs tracing along my stomach.

BEEP.

I followed through with the same movements, touching his warm skin.

BEEP.

He finally removed his mouth from mine, sharply inhaling.

"Mother fucker isn't going to stop."

BEEP.

He let out a slight snarl, squeezing my hips before turning his attention to dinner. I watched him remove the food, casually drinking a second glass with a smile.

"You spoil me," I mumbled.

"Well…someone has to," he quickly replied as he worked. "Go ahead and sit. I'll serve you, miss."

I took my seat and admired his table setting. He had a small bouquet in autumnal colors with a tiny pumpkin beside the vase and a wooden turkey.

"I didn't realize how domesticated you are." I turned the turkey around, admiring the trinket. It was goofy-looking. Perfect for Liam.

"Always thought I would make a great housewife someday." He set a small bowl before me containing a mixed salad of baby greens, tomatoes, and shredded carrots. "Lasagna is cooling."

"Thank you."

He sat across from me. The table was small, but the flowers blocked my view of him. I took a bite of my salad and held back a laugh as his hands suddenly appeared around the vase, sliding it across the table in a loud, vibrating manner.

"Didn't think that one through," he muttered.

"It's a nice setup, though. But it looks just as good off to the side."

Things fell into an awkward silence, and then Liam mumbled something beneath his breath as he scooted his chair to the right-hand side of mine. He sat closer, fed me a youthful grin, and drank his wine. The closer proximity helped. It felt more natural for us.

"So, how was Thanksgiving with your family?" I asked.

"Good, good. You know, the usual."

I could tell he didn't want to discuss it too much, and I reassured him. "Tell me all about it. I would like to hear what it's like."

"What it's like?"

"To…have a holiday with a somewhat healthy family."

Liam held back a moment, staring at his salad, then he cleared his throat and commenced a long tale about his family. He prattled as he served each course of our meal, leaving out no details about the traditions they had held since he was young. Most seemed normal, but some were unique to inside jokes and tales from his childhood. He laughed and smiled throughout the conversation, making me happy and hopeful that someday I could experience something like that.

"Your family sounds nice," I said as he served dessert. The brownies were a recipe he had learned from his mother.

"Eh, I guess so."

It always bothered me when people with healthy, ordinary families shrugged it off as if it was no big deal. Like those who would counter the stories of my childhood with, "Meh, everyone's family is weird" or "Mine isn't that great," when their upbringing was tremendously better and not filled with emotional and physical abuse. Obviously, life wasn't perfect for anyone.

Issues plagued everyone's family. But those who were blind to how blessed they were to have a loving home and parents who cheered them on and meant it when they said, "I love you," were somewhat irritating. Liam wasn't as bad as others I had known, but he was from a healthy household with parents who never divorced and cared for one another. He never went without food, lived in questionable conditions, or had to wear hand-me-downs. In a way, he was a bit spoiled, but he was never an asshole about it. Liam was the most caring and giving person I had ever known. And it was one of the things I loved most about him.

And for the cherry on top, Liam's mother was like a goddess compared to mine, and admittedly, I was jealous of it. I had the pleasure of meeting the woman once during one of her visits. His mother was incredibly gentle and kind, and her love for Liam and his siblings seemed out of this world. I wanted to be a mother someday but feared I wouldn't be good at it. I struggled with the idea of wanting to be better than what I had and the fear that I would become precisely what I didn't want to be—my mom.

"You okay?" he asked, shaking me from my thoughts.

"Yeah. Just…thinking."

"You've had a rough weekend."

"Mmm…yeah. I suppose so."

His hand covered mine, causing me to make eye contact. It made me feel shy, and I didn't quite know why. The dynamics of our relationship had shifted so much over the past few weeks in a way I did not expect. Whereas before, I wanted nothing intimate with Liam, now I found that it was a desire I had entertained a lot the past few days. He was intelligent, attractive, and great with children. He had a healthy family and had his head on straight, and suddenly, I felt like I was merely going to lose it all. I would never be able to hold onto and maintain something as wholesome as that.

"I…don't deserve you, Liam," I whispered.

"What are you talking about?"

"This. All of this. You."

He frowned. "You deserve everything you want, Zoey. Whatever that may be. I don't know what you truly wish for, but you should know I want you to have it. You seem off today, and it concerns me."

"It's because I don't know what I'm doing." Tears brimmed my eyes. I only wanted to be happy for him, yet I became depressed instead. Nobody could possibly want me in that state. Maybe I deserved people like Mysterious—dark, brooding, rough. "I'll be right back."

I went to the bathroom, taking the time to compose myself, angry for showing vulnerability around him, revealing the fear and negativity that so often disgusted those around me. As I opened the door, he met me in the hallway. Before I could say anything, his arms were around me, hugging me tightly.

"Don't hide from me, Zoey. I'm not like those people from your past. I care about you more than you know." He softly planted a kiss on my forehead. I exhaled and felt some of the tension release.

"Will I ever be good enough?" My voice sounded muffled against his shirt.

"You already are," he whispered. Of course, he always said the right things. A small whimper escaped, betraying me. "Okay, look at me. Look." He held my face, staring into my eyes with a stern expression. "You are smart, talented, funny, beautiful, and my best friend. You mean more to me than anyone else. You are good enough. You always have been and always will be. I know what you're thinking—that you're worthless and no good. Believe me, I've been there. I know those feelings. And it probably doesn't help to say that, but you have to know you're not alone. And even when the days feel like they are caving in on you, when you think you're unlovable, I'm here thinking you're the best damn woman I've ever known."

I bit my lip, unsure of what to say.

"And when you look at me like that…it drives me mad," he whispered.

A slight grin crossed my face.

"Oh, yup. That's the look. That's the one."

I blushed and giggled. "Quit it."

"Nope. Not gonna. Not gonna quit if it makes you smile." His tongue flicked over his lower lip before his teeth grazed the supple flesh.

We both moved, kissing once again as we forgot about dessert. Liam's caresses became needier but different than usual. Large hands stroked my face, slid down my sides, and then his thumbs trailed under my shirt to lightly touch my skin, tickling me. It seemed he was nervous in his movements, overly careful.

"Can…can I have you?" he asked.

"Yes," I immediately responded.

Liam led me to his room. It was dark save for the retro lava lamp at his bedside, which cast a soft blue light over his mattress. He faced me, planting kisses upon my lips and neck, his motions more confident. Lightly, I tugged on his jeans, my fingers dipping inside. A quiet noise escaped him as he pulled up my shirt, to which I allowed its complete removal as I did the same to his. He pressed another kiss firmly on my mouth and then lightly pushed me. I fell back onto the bed and crawled into the middle, eagerly waiting for him to join. He quickly undid his jeans, his belt unraveling with a snap as he tugged it away and crawled over me, pressing his lips against the sensitive spots on my throat and chest as he quickly pulled down my yoga pants.

"Quick and easy removal. I like that," he whispered as he plopped beside me, his tongue entering my mouth.

I wore no panties, and his fingers immediately slipped between my legs. Slick and sensitive, his light touches turned me on far more than the harder presses he usually did. His middle finger slid over the gap between my folds, making me gasp against his lips. I cupped his face, taking his tongue deep into my mouth. I nibbled his lower lip and slid my hands to the top of his jeans as he massaged my tender spot, teasing my entrance with light pressure. As soon as I gripped his erection, his movements paused as he watched me remove it from his pants. I rubbed him up and down, my thumb slipping over his head. His mouth hung open from the contact, his eyes large and lustful. He felt heavier than usual, thicker, twitching.

"Fuck, I'm so turned on right now," he huskily whispered.

Just hearing him say that in his natural voice turned me on.

"So wet," he said as he nibbled my earlobe.

I eyed his physique, admiring it for the first time. Mysterious always kept his clothing on. I had barely seen any part of him during our games. But now, as Liam, I could genuinely enjoy every bit of him. And I could tell this was also new and different for him. He appeared more vulnerable, and it made me feel more confident. He exhaled a low moan with closed eyes, his hips thrusting toward my hand.

"Keep it up much longer, and you're gonna make me cum," he hissed.

"Same." I could barely speak. Seeing Liam like this was extremely erotic.

His eyes opened, and he moved his fingers deep inside me, curling them faster and harder.

"Liam!" I gasped, grabbing his wrist. "I don't want to go yet."

He quickly removed his hand, chuckling. "It was too tempting."

I ran my fingers over his hardened cock faster for a second, glaring at him. "Yeah? Is this tempting?"

"Shit! Shit! Zoey!" he shouted with a laugh, removing my hands and rolling atop me. "You're going to kill me."

I giggled, liking the playful vibe. "Well…are you gonna slip it inside me so I can finish?"

He rolled his eyes, chewing his lip. "Impatient little brat."

I wiggled beneath him, feeding him an impish smile.

He held up a finger. "Wait." Leaning toward his nightstand, he opened the drawer and retrieved a black blindfold. "Shall we? To keep things…mysterious?" He raised an eyebrow.

I eyed the cloth, and it reminded me of how he had tied me down the night before. I didn't want that again. I wanted Liam, not Mysterious.

I shook my head. "No. Not this time." I guided my hand to his face. "I just want you."

He gave me a curious look and then a giant, lopsided grin. "Just me?"

"Yeah." I wrapped my legs around his waist. "Now, take off those pants and get inside of me."

He grunted in response, quickly removing his jeans as I kicked off mine hanging around my ankles and swiftly removed my bra. I barely finished before he dropped onto me, pressing his warm chest against mine. Hot, aching, twitching, his tip teased my entrance as he focused on my neck and breasts with his mouth. I played with his hair, my hips swirling beneath him. Liam was so much gentler this way, sensual. A shout escaped me as he suddenly pressed his mouth against me between my legs.

"Shit! Any more foreplay, and I'm gonna lose it."

He smiled, and I glared at him. His tongue plunged into me, and I tightly gripped his hands, which had settled on my thighs to keep them spread. So close. I was so close. I ground against his face, unable to maintain my breaths and noises. As I was about to reach release, he removed his mouth, wiped his chin, and crawled over me, kissing me. He made eye contact.

"Ready?" he asked.

I smirked. Why would he even ask such a thing? "Of course, I'm ready, you jerk."

With his mouth parted, he slid into me. I gasped, ready to explode, and bit back the desperate need. He was thick, hitting every space, it seemed. Perhaps it was because of the rough sex from the night before, but everything felt more sensitive and fuller. Liam groaned and lowered his head against my neck as he gently pulled out and sank further in. It felt wonderful. Everything about him was intoxicating.

Without much thought, I sighed with every movement he made. His hands slid down my arms, and just when I thought he would pin them above my head, he clasped his fingers around mine. We rocked together, nice and slow, enjoying each other's bodies. I squeezed around him from inside, and he made a loud noise of pleasure.

"You feel that?" I asked.

"Yeah, it's amazing," he said.

In retaliation, he slowed to a halt and flexed, smirking as he jerked inside me. We took turns squeezing and twitching, barely moving, enjoying the sensations. I was the first to give, rolling my hips beneath him, desperate to reach my peak and amazed I had lasted so long. As I quickened my pace, he clued in and did the same. His eyes lit up with interest and arousal as my breathing became frantic.

"Yes," I repeated over and over again as he adjusted his position and speed.

"Fuck," he muttered as I neared my climax.

My back arched as I came hard. I dug my nails into his arm, crying out in pleasure. It was one of the strongest orgasms I had had in a long time. Liam clenched his teeth and fell forward, convulsing over me as he also came. I wrapped my arms around him, kissing the side of his head, whispering in his ear as he finished his release. After a minute of us singing our pleasures to an end, he slid out and rested beside me, catching his breath.

"Well…" he started, "that was fun."

I curled up against him, resting on his chest. His arm wrapped around me, and he casually smooched my forehead.

"Hmm, yeah. I liked that a lot more than last night," I said tiredly.

A vibration sounded from the nightstand where his phone was plugged in. He ignored it.

"Hm? Last night?" He snorted a laugh. "Well, yeah…I can imagine anything would be better than what you went through yesterday."

I eyed him, nervous about bringing up our game.

His phone vibrated again.

"I mean…last night," I said slowly.

"What happened last night?"

I rolled my eyes. "About our game. It was a bit rough last night. I think, maybe, we should lay down some ground rules. I…I'm not sure I liked everything about that. At least, there are things we can experiment with, but maybe we should discuss it first."

He gave me a bewildered look. His phone hummed once again.

"What the hell is going on with my phone?" he snarled as he reached over and grabbed his cell. "I'm not sure I'm following you. About the game? You mean our sex game?"

"Yeah. I know we aren't supposed to talk about it, but I feel like, after last night, we should. Just to straighten things out."

Liam thumbed through his notifications. "Um, yeah, sure. I mean…if you want. Aw…no."

I tried to get a look at his phone. "What's wrong?"

"My sister…she just tagged me in all the photos from her daughter's birthday party."

I was confused. I thought Liam hadn't actually gone to the event. His sister lived hours away, and he still visited me that weekend.

"What do you mean?" I asked.

"Remember when she extorted me into dressing as a clown for my niece? After telling her not to, she thought it would be funny to tag me on every picture and video. Damnit…I need to play with my security settings, so she can't do that. So embarrassing."

He showed me his phone, and my heart locked up. Sure enough, he had been at the birthday party dressed as a clown.

"How on earth did you pull that off?"

"Pull what off?" he asked.

"You came to see me that night. You said you had to go out of town for that party and wouldn't be back to play our game. I was disappointed at first, but you still showed up. I thought you were lying about the birthday party so I wouldn't expect you," I explained.

His body shifted as he gaped at me with a look of wonder. He laughed and shook his head. "What are you talking about?"

"The excuses every weekend. I thought they were all lies to keep up the game's mystery."

"No, they weren't lies. Why would I lie about that stuff?"

I sat up and gazed at him. "I know I said we shouldn't discuss the game outside the bedroom, but time out. We definitely need to talk about it."

"Zoey, you're really confusing me right now. We haven't been able to play your little game because I have been so busy. I mean, there was one night I tried to come over, but the door was locked. I felt stupid, so I went home."

"What?" I stared at him, completely lost. Was he joking? Was he trying to play by my rules? "The makeup in your car. You've been using that to cover your face when you visit me at night."

Liam sat further away from me, acting a bit shielded. "I have no idea what in the hell you are talking about. I haven't visited you. That face paint was for my niece's birthday."

"The night of the museum! You saw me afterward!"

"No." Liam firmly shook his head, his expression making me angry. He looked at me like I was crazy.

"Every weekend since I've mentioned it, you've been over! We've been playing our game."

"Are you…like having wet dreams about me or something?" He chuckled, but it sounded a bit sarcastic.

"No more game! Reality, now. Forget anything I said about our rules; I need to know what's happening."

"Zoey…you're kind of freaking me out."

"Don't give me that look. Everyone gives me that look. Whether you're joking or not, don't treat me like I'm crazy," I snapped.

"I haven't been visiting you at night. I swear!"

I stood up, quickly putting on my clothes. "Where is the key I gave you?"

Liam frowned. "I…I don't have it. I'm sorry. I must have dropped it in the snow or somewhere in my car. I'll pay to have a new copy made."

"Are you for real?" I asked, not believing him.

"Yes."

"I don't like this. This isn't the kind of game I wanted to play! What you did last night was scary, Liam!"

"I didn't do anything! I was here cleaning my apartment!" He stood up as well, running his hands through his hair. "What is going on? Are you messing with me?"

"No! I think you're messing with me, though!"

I must've looked furious because he suddenly looked scared. "Shit, you're serious, aren't you?"

"Yeah, I'm fucking serious, Liam!"

He ran his hand over his face. A look of shock and dread overcame him. "Zoey," he carefully spoke, "are you taking your meds?"

My blood ran cold. There, in one instant, he became like everyone else. "Why would you say that to me?" I whispered, rage filling my soul.

"Cuz you are acting a bit…." he paused.

"Crazy?! Am I acting crazy, Liam?!" I couldn't breathe as panic overwhelmed my senses. Maybe he was a psycho. I stood in the room for what felt like an eternity—numb, cold, aching. I had no idea how long we remained frozen like that. Suddenly, blind rage took over. "Fuck! I knew this was a bad idea! Screw you, you gaslighting mother fucker!"

I stomped into the living room and grabbed my coat and purse. Liam fumbled after me as he struggled to throw on some clothes. I didn't wait and dashed into the stairwell, heading straight for the parking lot.

"Zoey!" I could hear him as he exited his apartment and sprinted down the stairs. "Zoey, wait! Wait! We need to talk! We *have* to talk!"

"I don't want to talk to you, Liam! You messed it all up!" I screamed, slipping on the ice. I balanced myself on one of the vehicles in the parking lot. I looked back and saw him jump down the last few steps, rushing toward me. I made a strange noise as I carefully ran to my car, but he caught up with me before I could get in. I grabbed the handle, and he pressed against the door, preventing me from opening it.

"Please! Stop! Something weird is going on, and we need to discuss this," he heaved. He was shirtless and without shoes, his breath fogging before his face.

I pushed away from him, walking into the middle of the parking lot. "I don't think there's anything else to discuss. The game's over. We aren't doing this anymore."

"Zoey." He sighed. "Please. I swear to God. I have not been over to your place at night. That," he pointed toward his apartment, "was the first time we have ever had sex. If you're not playing with me, then there is seriously something weird going on, and we need to figure out—"

Tires squealed on the pavement. The roar of a car speeding down the lot tore my attention away from Liam. Its lights flashed bright, blinding me.

"Zoey! Get out of the way!" Liam dashed and pushed me just as the car nearly crashed into me.

I fell onto the sludgy road, rolling. I had never been shoved so hard in my life. My neck hurt, and my entire body ached from the impact with the asphalt. Another screech from the tires distracted me from the pain. The driver was long gone, speeding onto the highway. I gaped where I had been standing and screamed. Liam lay face down in the parking lot, his face covered in blood. I crawled to him and lightly touched his shoulder. He made no movement nor sound.

"LIAM!"

CHAPTER ELEVEN

LIAM

An excruciatingly loud alarm brought me from the darkness that clouded my mind. My body jostled back and forth, each fiber of my being throbbing with pain. The headache I had was worse than any migraine I'd experienced before. I felt like I was going to vomit.

"He's awake," a voice shouted above me.

Slowly, I opened my eyes. The bright lights only made my head pound worse, and I closed my eyes again, licking my dry lips. I tasted blood. It took a moment before I realized what was happening around me.

"Sir. Sir! Can you hear me?" the voice asked.

"Hrm, yeah," I groaned. Speaking hurt.

"Sir, can you tell me your name."

"Liam. Liam DeCarlo."

"Liam. You were hit by a car. Do you remember anything before the accident?"

I thought hard for a moment, stunned by everything happening around me. "Car accident? I wasn't…driving."

"You weren't driving. It was an auto-ped accident. You were hit in the parking lot."

"Parking lot," I muttered. Utter fright washed over me as I suddenly remembered what had happened. "Zoey! Is she okay? I was with a woman named Zoey."

"She's just fine. She's following right behind us in her car. She was adamant she came with you," the paramedic explained.

I relaxed a bit, knowing that Zoey was safe.

"Do you know who it was that hit you?"

I shook my head and winced. A C-collar was around my neck. I had no idea who would have been behind the wheel outside of a crazy drunk. "No."

"Your friend seemed confused and greatly concerned. She could not tell who it was either."

The ambulance took me to the nearest hospital. I went through a thorough examination and took a couple of X-rays. I lay in bed, feeling loopy from the morphine in my system. I tried not to move my arm too much. It had swelled quite a bit, possibly broken. My jaw hurt, but the medics were sure it was fine. Somehow, my legs survived the brunt of the hit. When I pushed Zoey, I jumped just right where I landed on the hood and windshield of the vehicle and rolled up and over the top. The pain in my head was from the pavement, which led to a few stitches and a bad concussion. Eventually, they moved me to a private room, where the doctor confirmed I no longer needed the C-collar. As he removed it, there came a knock at the door. A nurse entered, and Zoey rushed in.

"Liam. Are you okay? What's going on?" She looked frantic, her eyes swollen and red.

"Liam is going to be fine. He's lucky he was hit in a parking lot and not the street. Most likely, the speed at which the car was traveling had been relatively low. How he'd been hit wasn't as detrimental as it could have been. And being in good health, Liam only sustained a sprained wrist and a few stitches on his head, and the rest of his injuries include minor scratches and bruising. There are no internal injuries, bleeding, or fractures, but he'll be very sore in the coming days. Don't be surprised to find some nasty bruising in the future," The doctor said as he read the chart. "He's been here long enough that I believe sending him home is safe, even with that concussion. Can you keep an eye on him, or does he have someone to watch over him?"

Zoey moved toward my bed, dropping into the seat beside me. "Yes, I will stay with him."

"Good. A nurse should be in soon to give you home care instructions. Please take a couple of days to rest. Call us immediately if you notice any more swelling, anywhere at all, dizziness, or trouble with your vision or mental state."

"Will do. Thanks," Zoey said.

"Thank you, doctor," I muttered. I was exhausted.

"Stay awake!" Zoey snapped. I hadn't realized I had shut my eyes. The doctor chuckled as he left the room. As soon as the door closed, Zoey scooted closer to me, whispering my name.

I eyed her, giving her a dopey smile. My vision had bettered over the past few hours, but I was sure sheer exhaustion caused me to see two of her. "Hey…Lil Zoey."

She grabbed my left hand, the one not wrapped. "I was so scared. Worried that you had been killed."

"Naw," I tried to laugh, but it hurt. "Not gonna die anytime soon."

"I'm sorry, Liam."

"For what? You didn't do anything."

Tears fell from her eyes. "I feel like all of this is my fault. God, it's just been one thing after another. I wish you hadn't pushed me out of the way; you would have been fine!"

A spike of irritation spread throughout me. "No, Zoey. If you had been hit, I think you would have been in far worse shape. I wouldn't dare risk that. I would hate myself forever if I allowed that to happen."

She heaved a massive sigh, her head hanging low.

"Hey," I shook her hand. "You look beat."

She sniffed and looked up. "I am exhausted, but I must stay awake for you."

"How long have I been here?" I asked.

Zoey gazed at her phone. "Phone's dead." She eyed the clock on the wall. "Well, it's nearly 2 am. It's been a long time."

I wasn't sure when the car hit me, but I remembered we had started dinner around five.

"Once that nurse finally shows up, I'll take you home. I'll be staying with you at your place to keep an eye on you. I will text Maria and call her in the morning so she knows what's up," she said.

Good old Zoey and her motherly instincts. "You don't have to stay with me," I reassured her.

"I'm staying. I'm not leaving you alone with a concussion and the possibility of things getting worse. What if they missed something?" she worried.

"Don't make me paranoid, woman. Sheesh."

The door opened, and a male nurse entered the room. "Liam?" he asked in a muffled voice behind a surgical mask.

"Yeah. That's me."

The nurse strolled forward with a syringe and a clipboard. He paused and gazed upon Zoey. "I'm sorry, but visiting hours are over."

"Oh, but I'm taking him home," she replied.

"He's staying overnight," the nurse quickly interrupted her.

"The doctor said I could leave, that everything checked out," I said in an even tone. I didn't appreciate this guy's rudeness.

"There was something on the CT scan. We need to keep you overnight for observation. We will call your friend in the morning if that's your preferred contact," he muttered, reading the paperwork.

"Oh, um…okay." Zoey looked at me with concern. "He's going to be okay, right?"

"Yes, just fine as long as nothing worsens." The nurse eyed her. Though you couldn't see his face, you could read the scowl through his eyes. "We have lots of patients tonight, so I need to treat him with this morphine and get on to the next room, but I need to make sure you leave first. Policy and all that."

"Right. Right." Zoey turned to me and gently kissed my cheek. "Message me all night if you must. Let me know you're okay."

"Will do." I squeezed her hand.

She quickly said goodbye and left the room. The nurse stared at the door, even long after the woman left. I adjusted myself in bed. I didn't feel too bad. The last set of morphine had been more than enough. Besides, I didn't like having too many drugs in my system.

"Hey, uh, if it's all good, I don't think I need more pain meds. I barely feel a thing as it is."

The nurse turned toward me; his eyes were wide, his pupils thin. He didn't respond for a long while. Okay, things were beginning to get a bit odd. I had heard doctors and nurses could be cold and sometimes mean, but this guy gave me the creeps. The man stepped back and slowly locked the door with a loud 'click.'

"Hey, man…what's going on?" I asked, eyeing the room for some form of protection.

"Oh…don't worry…this isn't morphine."

Shit, shit, shit! My mind reeled. This was some scary movie shit.

I struggled to move out of bed, and then the dizziness overcame me. The man moved closer, dropping the clipboard while raising the syringe. I tried to look for a nametag but found none.

"Get the fuck away from me!" I shouted.

"You can't have her! She's mine. She's MINE!" the crazed man shouted as he lunged for me.

"What the hell are you talking about?!" I rolled out of bed just as the man readied to stab me with the syringe. The needle plunged deep into my pillow instead. I hit the floor hard, but luckily, the meds in my system prevented me from feeling much, but I knew I was going to hurt worse in the morning.

"You can't have her!" he screamed and slid over the bed, reaching for me.

"Help! Somebody help!" I frantically crawled around the bed frame, trying to get my legs underneath me. My heart pounded in my chest, and everything in the room spun from the sudden movement. I felt nauseous and weak. The man ran into me, tackling me. His hands immediately flew to my throat, squeezing. I fought beneath him, pushing to get away. With each scoot, I slid closer a couple of inches to the opposite side of the bed where the table and utensils had scattered to the floor. My fingers clawed at the man's hands. I had nothing to look at other than his crazed eyes.

"She's mine. She's mine. She…she loved me, not you!"

"Who…the fuck…are you?" I asked as I drove my left fist into the man's face. It was enough to knock him off balance. I scrambled to my hands and knees, adrenaline kicking in, and crawled to the call button dangling over the side of the bed. I pressed it just as the nurse leaped onto my back, punching me in the head.

"Zoey…is mine!" he screamed.

It all clicked. This man was obsessed with Zoey. He had to be the guy who had hit me with the car. I felt sick to my stomach as I suddenly realized something else. Zoey wasn't lying. A man was visiting her in the middle of the night, only it wasn't me. It had to be this crazy bastard.

I screamed and rolled backward with all my rage, slamming myself on top of the man. I turned and punched him square in the jaw with my good hand and ripped off his mask. My body froze as I gazed at the mysterious man's face.

"You?" I asked, breathing heavily.

Our eyes locked, and for the first time, I recognized the man I had seen numerous times in the past. He had brown hair like mine. His eyes were bluer than my grey ones, but they could easily be hidden at night or with contact lenses. I eyed his torso and the rest of his physique. We were of similar shape and size. He was a bit thinner than me, but the form of his face was also a close match. I didn't know how the guy could pull it off, but if face paint was involved, I could speculate he looked enough like me to fool even Zoey.

Some staff knocked and shouted outside the door, the handle rattling. I chanced a glance away, and the guy sucker-punched me hard, sending me back in a daze.

"If I can't have her, nobody can!" he raged as he ran for the door, unlocked it, and sped out into the hall, shoving past the nurses. Numerous shouts and screams followed, and a security guard appeared in the doorway.

I scrambled to my feet. "Get him!"

"Are you okay?" the large man asked.

"Fuck me! Go after him! He's dangerous!" I screamed.

The security guard took off, shouting into his radio. A nurse filed in, looking me over. I walked around the room, searching for my cell phone and clothes.

"Sir, I need you to lie back down. You're in no condition to be moving around so much. I need to make sure you're okay after that attack," the woman said.

"I don't have time. He's going to go after her," I said, pulling up Zoey's number. The phone went straight to voicemail. "Shit!"

"Please, sir. Let me examine you! Sir!"

I rushed out of the room, running down the hall, calling Zoey again before dialing for a ride. I had to get there as soon as possible.

CHAPTER TWELVE

ZOEY

I drove home slowly, listening to calming music. My mind was everywhere but where it needed to be. Luckily, there weren't many cars on the road. I felt numb. The past few days had been a rollercoaster of drama mixed with trauma, and I couldn't get over the fact that I had to leave Liam behind. I didn't like it. It didn't feel right.

I approached my apartment with disdain, unsure what to think or feel. We just had our first fight, and then a car slammed into Liam and hospitalized him. Yes, I felt awful, but couldn't stop thinking about our argument. Was he for real, or was he taking the game too seriously? One thing was for sure: we weren't playing Codename: Mystery anymore. My mind fought with my exhaustion. Even though I was tired, I knew I wouldn't be able to sleep. The only thing keeping me going in the right direction was Hector.

I entered my apartment, and a quiet mew greeted me from the couch. I tried to turn the living room light on, but it wouldn't work. I growled with frustration. As I stepped forward, something crunched beneath my shoes. I eyed the floor and could make out a bit of broken glass. Had the bulb blown out? It was strange.

"Weird things are happening today, Hector."

I moved to the sofa and lightly touched the cat, giving him a hug and a big kiss on his soft head between his ears. A deep purr rumbled from him.

"Let's head to bed, Bubba. I'm not even hungry." I had laid out enough food for him in case I stayed too late over at Liam's. I eyed the bowl in the kitchen and noticed there was enough to last him the night if he needed a snack, but around this time, he was usually curled up with me in the bedroom anyway.

I moved to the back of the apartment, plugging my phone into my charger by my nightstand. I stared at it for a second before I turned it on. As the phone lit up, a multitude of notifications flickered on the screen, all from Liam. My blood ran cold. Had I missed something?

I brought the phone up to my face, adjusting the blinding light. I had four missed calls, each with a voicemail, and numerous texts.

'Don't go home! Get out of there!'

"What the fuck?" I muttered as I scrolled through the others.

'I called the police; get out!'

'Call me as soon as you can!'

'Are you at home?! Call me!'

'The nurse was crazy! Get out!'

Before I could read them all, a call came in from Liam's cell. I quickly answered.

"Hello? Liam?"

"ZOEY! Oh my god! Where are you?"

"I'm at my apartment. I just got here."

"No! Get out!"

"Liam, what's going on? I can't leave, or my phone will die. It's on the charger."

"I don't care! Get out! You have a crazy stalker, Zoey!"

"What are you talking about?"

"I'm on the way. I called the police. They should be there soon!"

The heater kicked on, and the curtains in my bedroom fluttered, allowing some light into the room only for a flickering moment. Something moved from the corner of my room, and I faced it.

"Goddamn it, Liam…what is this bullshit?" I asked, lowering the cell phone.

"Zoey! Get out!" Liam's voice screamed from the phone in my hand.

The silhouette in the corner of the room remained silent, unmoving, watching me from the shadows. I swallowed hard, every hair on my body standing on end as my nerves turned ice-cold. I quickly lifted the cell to my ear.

"Liam?" I whispered. "Is that you?"

The figure stepped forward, tearing the curtain away to allow more light into the room. It was Mysterious. He donned all-black clothing, his hood drawn, but his makeup was a messy smear of colors hiding his face. While lifting his hand into the light, he pinched a small silver item between his fingers—my apartment key.

"Is he there? Get the hell out of there!" Liam cried out.

Something silver and much larger glinted in Mysterious' other hand. He held a knife.

"I told you to stay away from him!" Mysterious suddenly shouted at me.

"LIAM!" I shrieked and dropped the phone just as the man made a mad dash for me.

I made it to the living room, and a quick glance confirmed that the baseball bat I kept by the entry was now missing. As I reached for the door, the man forced it closed. A scream escaped my lips, and I immediately backpedaled, narrowly avoiding a slash to my gut. I hopped over the sofa and ran into the kitchen. I had to get something, anything. Hector darted out of the way, and

I was glad, hoping he hid under the bed. If anything were to happen to him, I would kill a mother fucker.

My apartment was small, so it didn't take much for Mysterious to catch up with me. As I reached for my set of knives, his blade cut across my arm. I quickly retracted and spun. I had no gun, and my pepper spray remained inside my purse in the bedroom. He would undoubtedly catch me before I retrieved it. As I turned, a little green light caught my attention. The coffee pot had been left on all day and still held some of my morning brew. I grabbed the small pot and turned as he slashed me across my side. With a cry, I threw the hot coffee right into his face. His hands immediately reached for his eyes, and I smashed the glass pot over his head as he wildly swung his knife, the blade catching my thigh. We both dropped to the floor, and I tried to return to my feet. I slipped on the hot liquid and turned as he gripped me, snatching a shard of glass for defense.

With a wild scream, I cut into the spot between his neck and shoulder. It wasn't a large piece of glass, but it was enough to distract him. Pain be damned, I had enough! I shoved him back, crawled over him, and fought for the knife in his hand. I had no idea how to overpower him, but I grabbed it with all my might, grasping the blade to twist it at an odd angle, hoping he would lose grip. He jerked it to the side as he punched me in the ribs, the blade cutting deeply into my palm, but I held back a scream as I stood a little higher and dropped my knee right into his crotch. That did it.

He released the blade, and, despite all my feelings, I forced myself to attack him. I didn't want to stab anyone. The idea had always sounded awful to me. I never wanted to know what it felt like or looked like. Like stepping on a hard-shelled bug, where you could still feel it through your shoe, the idea made me cringe. But it took only a split second to decide it was all or nothing. I was not going to die tonight because of some crazed lunatic. I raised the knife into the air as his hand gripped my throat. Releasing another feral scream, I willed myself to follow through and plunged the blade directly into his chest.

Mysterious made a slight noise, his eyes widening enough that I could see the white even in the dark room. I pulled the knife out of his body with a cry and sank it deep a second time. His hands flailed to mine, and he gurgled a strange sound as he looked at me.

This was Mystery—a strange, dark, twisted fantasy that was dangerous and mesmerizing. All this time, I had thought he was Liam. Now, I had no idea who he was, and it made me feel sick. I felt lightheaded, close to fainting. From afar, I could hear sirens approaching. I leaned forward, looking into his eyes.

"Z…Zoe…." he tried to talk, raising his hand toward my face. I quickly batted it away, gritting my teeth as tears covered my cheeks.

I sniffed. "Just…die!" I harshly whispered.

He trembled beneath me, his mouth opening and closing as he tried to breathe and speak. His fingers held onto my hand.

"My…mine," he choked.

I growled, removed the knife from him again, and prepared to give a final blow. But as I pulled it away from his chest, blood rippled onto the floor, and a sharp exhale escaped him, crimson seeping from his mouth, mixing with the paint on his face. Carefully, I watched him for a moment, ensuring he remained still. Blood soaked through my pants, and I gasped, pushing away with the knife still clutched in my hand.

A loud bang sounded as someone rushed through my front door.

"Zoey!" It was Liam.

I couldn't say anything; my voice caught in my throat. I heard him dash to my bedroom, calling my name repeatedly. Then, he approached the kitchen, stopping at the sight of the body on the floor.

"Liam," I finally whispered.

"Holy shit! Zoey! Are you all right? Are you all right!?" He leaped over the man and kneeled on the floor, wrapping his arms around me.

"He…he's dead, right?" I could barely manage the words, but I needed to know.

Liam stared at him. His heart pounded in my ear as he scooped me closer to him, shielding me with his arms. "Yes," he finally spoke.

"Who…was he?" I wasn't sure I wanted to know.

"Remember the med student Ronnie hired at the bar a month ago?"

Memories of the new employee breaking glasses, bringing us our orders late, and asking if we needed anything else rushed through my mind. He had listened to our conversations.

"He heard us talk about the game," I whispered.

Liam covered my head, planting a kiss atop my hair.

And then I remembered the news reports of the months leading up to the game. Women throughout the city were attacked, raped, and some even murdered—by stabbing. I felt numb to the situation around me. The police arrived seconds later, but I didn't process what was happening or what was said to me. I couldn't speak or move and remained locked in Liam's embrace. Through his arms, I looked sideways at the body on the floor. I now knew his face but still didn't know his name.

I had gotten a taste of the mysterious things in this world. And they were nothing but trouble.

3 Months Later

"Liam! Where do you want these boxes?" I yelled as I shuffled into our new apartment. Carrying two boxes at once was a bad idea.

"In the bedroom!" he shouted.

I grunted with each step as I heaved our belongings into the back room.

"Woah! What are you doing, crazy? You're going to hurt yourself!" Liam helped me set the boxes on the floor.

"They were the last two. I didn't want to make another trip. I'm tired," I whined.

"I could have gotten them, silly."

"You're too busy playing with everything you unwrap; it would have taken another hour to do it."

He rolled his eyes. "Did you close everything up?"

"Yeah. The car's locked. All done. Now, all we got to do is unpack everything." I jumped onto the bed, letting out a content sigh. Hector dashed onto the mattress with an enthusiastic meow, falling into a balled position by my pillow. He thought it was nap time. Liam sank beside me.

After the incident with Mysterious, Liam and I only grew closer. He healed nicely despite a few unpleasant scars, as did my wounds. We went to therapy together, and he kept his phone on him at all times in case I needed him for anything, which ended up being a consistent ordeal with the recurring nightmares I suffered from the attack. Eventually, he opted to stay with me every night, petting me to sleep and whispering with reassurance that I was safe. And I did feel safe while he was nearby.

Once the police confirmed the man's identity, I ignored all reports and activities involving the ordeal. Even Maria was respectful enough not to bother me about it for a story. In fact, Liam handled all the talking. I didn't care who the man was, where he came from, or why he was the way he was. I wanted to forget about those weeks and the incidents that occurred. I had the scars as a reminder, and it was hard enough facing that every single day. No, I had enough of Mysterious and never planned on returning to those memories for as long as I could stand. My future was all I cared about.

"Wanna order a pizza?" Liam asked.

"Damnit, I'm trying to lose weight," I complained. He eyed me, and after a second, I agreed. "Okay, fine."

He clapped his hands. "Okay, great! I will order cheesy bread, too."

"I hate you," I laughed.

He rolled over me, pressing his nose against mine. "I thought you loved me," he said in an annoying voice he often used while mimicking the puppets on television.

"Only when you don't use that awful voice," I said.

He laughed as he kissed me and tickled my sides. I shrieked with laughter and then hissed a small 'ow.' He abruptly stopped and lifted my shirt, gently kissing the new scar on my side. Even though it had healed, it still ached when touched at times.

"I'm sorry, sweetheart," he whispered, planting his lips across my belly.

"Liam." I ran my fingers through his hair. He went higher, lifting my shirt more. "Liam." He kept going, smooching my cleavage and then my collarbone. "Liam!"

A quick succession of kisses covered my neck, cheeks, and then my lips. "What?" he cheekily asked.

"Order that damn pizza; I'm starving," I huffed.

One more kiss on the lips, and he said, "Okay."

He hopped out of bed and sashayed in a goofy way into the other room, retrieving his phone. I giggled at his weird antics. He had been in a good mood since I agreed to move into an apartment with him. A new complex, a new layout, nothing about this location reminded me of my old home. And having him nearby was comforting. Liam was the opposite of Mysterious, which was what I loved most about him.

ABOUT THE AUTHOR

A. R. Redington is a number one Audible and Amazon best-selling author. Born and raised in Kansas, she thrived creatively at an early age, focusing on art and storytelling. Her passion for gaming and character design led her to pursue an artistic career. She attended the Rocky Mountain College of Art + Design, receiving a BFA in illustration/children's book specialization. With experience in graphic design, formatting, illustration, editing, publishing, and writing, Redington creates and designs everything for her novels while working freelance on the side.

She is the author and illustrator of the sci-fi/fantasy series The Esoteric Design, Masters of the Ellem (fantasy), Trouble with Mystery (romantic thriller), Whispers from Beyond: 30 Miniature Tales (horror), and "The Trophy" from Predator: Eyes of the Demon. You can learn more about Redington at her website: www.ARRedington.com.